A TRAITOR AMONG US

A Traitor among Us

Elizabeth Van Steenwyk

EERDMANS BOOKS FOR YOUNG READERS
GRAND RAPIDS, MICHIGAN / CAMBRIDGE, U.K.

© 1998 Donald & Elizabeth Van Steenwyk Family Trust
Published 1998 by
Eerdmans Books for Young Readers
an imprint of
Wm. B. Eerdmans Publishing Co.
255 Jefferson Ave. S.E., Grand Rapids, Michigan 49503 /
P.O. Box 163, Cambridge CB3 9PU U.K.

Paperback edition 1999

Printed in the United States of America

03 02 01 00 99   7 6 5 4 3 2

Library of Congress Cataloging-in-Publication Data

Van Steenwyk, Elizabeth.
A traitor among us / by Elizabeth Van Steenwyk.
p.   cm.
Summary: In occupied Holland in 1944, thirteen-year-old Pieter
becomes increasingly involved in the work of the Dutch Resistance
even though he knows the risk of being discovered
by the Nazi informer who lives in his village.
ISBN 0-8028-5157-6 (pkb. : alk. paper).
1. World War, 1939-1945 — Netherlands — Juvenile fiction.
[1. World War, 1939-1945 — Netherlands — Fiction.
2. Netherlands — History — German occupation,
1940-1945—Fiction.]   I. Title.
PZ7.V358Tr   1998
[Fic] — dc21   97-14256
                                            CIP
                                            AC

For Don,
my favorite Dutchman

Contents

This is a story that could have happened. Although its characters are fictional, some of them were inspired by real people who fought and died in a place that is also real. This story is dedicated to their memory.

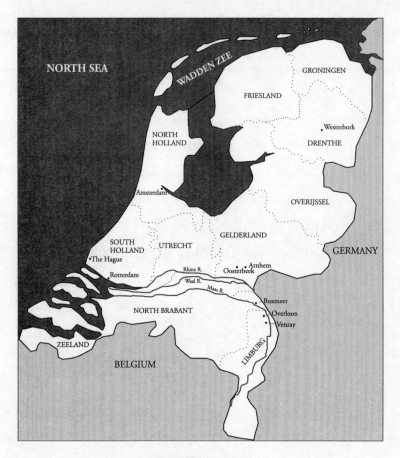

NETHERLANDS

Dorthwijk, located between Venray and Boxmeer
in this story, is an "invented" village, a composite
of many of the villages of the era.

CHAPTER 1

Bent Smokes

Saturday, September 16, 1944
Dorthwijk, the Netherlands

Fear pounded like a giant hammer inside Pieter's head. Any moment the Nazis would arrive, and he would die out here along the railroad tracks. People were shot for doing less than what he was going to do, had done for the last several weeks. He couldn't breathe. There wasn't room inside him for anything but the pounding fear. No room at all for air so he could breathe.

He should be used to it by now. The Nazis had been here for more than four years. Why couldn't he get used to the fear they brought with them?

What was that? It was so hard to see anything in the dark. There it was again, something touching his skin. Then he knew.

Calm down, Pieter, he told himself. It's only a blade of grass on your cheek. You're lying on grass, remember? Keep your wits about you. But it was so hard to wait for the Number 503 to come. There was always the risk that he'd be caught.

"Moffen." He whispered the word to fill himself with the rage it brought. The Dutch had branded the Nazis that when they came and brought the fear. "I'll get you, Moffen. One day, I'll get you."

There, that was better. He was still afraid, but now he was angry too, and that pushed out some of the fear.

He jumped as he felt a hand on his arm. The tall grass whispered as he whirled around. "Jan," he almost spoke aloud. "Don't creep up like that."

"I thought I heard you talking." Jan spoke so softly.

"It was nothing." Pieter parted the grass to look down the track. "I hate it when the train is late."

"Think of something else." Good old Jan, always trying to help.

"Food. I can always think of food." Pieter's stomach began to rumble, or maybe it was one continuous rumble now. He was always hungry. Had there ever been a time when he wasn't? "It's taking so long," he half-whispered.

"What is? The train?"

"Yes, that, and the war. It's taking forever."

"I know. We'll be old men, pensioners, before it's over." Jan sighed. "Any news?"

Pieter knew what he meant. "No." Jan was asking about Pieter's father, arrested by the Nazis a year ago. And Menno and Gerrit too, fighting with the Resistance. He'd always thought of his older brothers as heroes, and now they were.

2

But Pieter was thinking of Kazan too, his Belgian shepherd, his best friend. They had gone everywhere together since Papa brought him home the birthday that Pieter turned eight. There'd been a red bow tied to a cheese basket, and inside was a fat, cuddly black-and-white puppy. He'd jumped into Pieter's arms, and they'd been inseparable from then on. Sometimes Kazan had followed him to school and come back for him in the afternoon. And always, he had slept by Pieter's bed, a warm, comforting presence in the night as well.

A sob clotted in a hard knot in Pieter's throat until he thought it would choke him. Why had the Germans taken his dog, too?

He remembered the early days of the occupation when the Nazis ordered all dogs to be "registered" at headquarters. It was unreal, unbelievable. If the dogs were old, the owners could keep them, provided the dogs wore red tags. But all the strong ones were taken away. Pieter didn't register Kazan and only let him out at night, to pee. Even then he wore a red tag Mama had made.

But someone knew and told the Nazis. Maybe it was the same rat who told about his father's forbidden radio. No maybes. Pieter knew there was a traitor in the village.

"Listen. What was that rustling noise?"

"I didn't hear anything," Jan said. "You're so jumpy."

Pieter felt shaky inside too, as though his bones and skin were somehow disconnecting.

"The train is coming," Jan whispered.

They listened as the train screeched around a curve, brakes grabbing the rails. The blackout cloth over the headlight kept speed to a minimum. But no one was in a hurry on that train. German soldiers on their way to guard duty, civilians returning from back-breaking jobs. Who wanted to hurry anyway?

The train halted a few meters down the tracks, then doors opened and trash was dumped. A few weeks ago, Pieter and Jan had discovered this dump stop, and now it kept them and their families from starving. German trash keeps us alive, Pieter thought bitterly.

Jan poked Pieter, and he nodded. Something was different tonight. The train stayed still, unmoving. Pieter risked a glance through the grass and felt his insides twist like live things. A couple of soldiers had jumped down from the train, spewing gravel in their path as they walked. Cones of light crisscrossed above Jan and Pieter's heads as the soldiers headed slowly in their direction. Had they been seen?

"What shall we do?" Jan's whisper sounded desperate. Pieter motioned for silence, wondering if the throb in his temple would somehow make a sound and give them away. Sweat trickled down his shirt front, and he felt wet all over. He hadn't wet himself, had he? Wouldn't the Moffen love that, a thirteen-year-old . . .

The soldiers stopped nearby and turned their flashlights down the tracks. They seemed to be watching, waiting for something. A signal, perhaps.

Then Pieter remembered hearing the rumors that

4

the Resistance was at work nearby. Maybe the train had become a target. Made sense. There was a bridge ahead. Perfect place for a Resistance ambush. The Germans must be waiting for a safety check before proceeding.

Pieter dared to part the grass. Yes, that must be it. Signal lights flicked on, then off, then on again. The soldiers grunted something in low, guttural German and quickly returned to the train. Moments later it accelerated down the tracks.

As soon as the train was out of sight, Pieter stood on shaky legs, always dreading this moment. Was someone still nearby, ready to pounce, ready to drag him and Jan off to be shot? He held his breath and waited.

But Jan didn't wait. Instead he hurried down the gravel path beside the tracks toward the trash. Pieter followed in the near darkness.

"I hate this." Jan kicked at some stuff lying in a heap. "I hate poking through all this crap." They had to use their hands to find the smokes. Even if they'd had a flashlight, they couldn't risk using it.

"I hate being hungry." Pieter tried not to breathe in the stench as he pawed through the mess of papers and garbage. Sometimes he and Jan got lucky and found heaps of cigarette stubs in one place. Other times they had to sift through each scrap of garbage and dig for every butt.

"Good," Jan said, after a moment. "I found a bunch of them together." He pulled a well-mended sock from his pocket and began to fill it.

Bent smokes. That's what everyone called them, the stubs of cigarettes ground out by Germans and thrown out for desperate people to salvage. Like me, Pieter thought. I'm desperate enough to paw through this trash so Mama and I can trade the smokes for food. Slowly Pieter's spare sock began to fill too.

"That's it. We've got them all." Pieter stood up, then brushed dirt and gravel from the knees of his patched pants.

"How much do you think we have?" Jan asked.

"Enough for a little while." Pieter led the way down the path through the grass. Tomorrow he'd know for sure, after he broke open the cigarette paper and emptied the tobacco into Mama's butter crock. It hadn't contained butter for four years. The baker would take one pinch for a loaf of bread, the greengrocer four pinches for a few extra potatoes and some moldy carrots.

"Chocolate," Jan whispered. "I wonder if there's enough tobacco in the world to get some chocolate?"

Pieter wanted to laugh, but he couldn't get the sound out. Maybe he'd forgotten how. Then he heard that rustling noise again. He stopped so suddenly that Jan ran into him.

"Pieter . . ." Jan sounded cross.

"I heard it again," Pieter whispered. "Something over there. I know it." He began to shake inside again. They'd get caught, if not now, then soon.

"What will the Nazis do to a couple of kids out after curfew?" Jan asked.

But he knew, and so did Pieter. Their nerves were raw with the knowing.

"You keep walking," Pieter whispered. "Talk as if I'm there beside you, while I stay back to see who it is." Finding out would be better than waiting, than not knowing.

"Be careful," Jan whispered.

"I'm always careful. Nothing's going to happen." That was so ridiculous it was almost funny. Any moment something could happen. He'd been living with that knowledge since the Nazis came. Maybe that moment had arrived right now.

CHAPTER 2

Found Out

A moment later

Pieter dropped softly to his knees in the tall grass while Jan moved on, talking as if Pieter were still beside him. Hambone, that's what Jan was. He'd make a good actor one day, if the Nazis gave them a chance to grow up. Moffen. It was always the Moffen. They filled every waking thought with their rotten presence.

Pieter listened as the footsteps crunched closer, and he tensed for what might happen next. Waiting was hardest. It weighed his fear down until he felt flattened by it.

Was that a Nazi back there? Or was it the traitor from the village? Whoever he was, why didn't he make himself known? Was he waiting to take them with their families too? What would they do to Mama? The stories of how Nazis treated women were too real not to be true. He couldn't let that happen. He had to create a diversion, draw the Nazi away so Jan could escape, warn their families. Then Mama would be safe.

Pieter's neck and shoulders ached with the tension now. If only the fight were fair, he might have a chance. But nothing was fair during a war. He'd learned that early. Fair didn't exist anymore.

The footsteps drew closer as Pieter hugged the earth, its dampness soothing to his touch. Now the footsteps were nearly upon him, and he still didn't know what to do. The element of surprise — maybe that would work. It was all he had.

Pieter leapt up, feeling muscle spasms cramp his legs while the smell of onions nearly knocked him flat. Onions. Food.

"Eeee, yi! You scared me, Pieter. You're bad."

"Shut up, Koos." He breathed a huge sigh. "Do you want to bring the entire German regiment from Overloon?" Pieter whispered fiercely. He stared at Koos in the dimness, wondering how his dumb cousin could be smart enough to follow anyone, even this clumsily. Dumb? He wasn't so dumb; he'd eaten tonight. He had food in his belly, even if it was only onions.

"Do you think somebody heard me?" Koos glanced around. "I don't want to get in trouble."

"I heard you," Jan whispered, coming up to them. "Keep your voices down."

"You're not going to get in trouble." Pieter gave Koos a slight push. "Let's go home."

Obediently Koos began to walk ahead of Pieter and Jan, his blond hair a halo on his round head. Suddenly he turned. "You tricked me. I thought you had gone ahead, with Jan. But you were waiting to scare me."

"We had to see who you were," Jan said.

"But you still tricked me. I won't forget." Koos began to stumble through the coarse grass again.

It isn't hard to trick you, Pieter thought. My poor, stupid cousin. Mama said not to think of him that way, that he was just slow. He couldn't help it. But he'd been smart enough to follow them tonight.

"Koos." Pieter grabbed his arm and turned him around. The smell of his breath made Pieter's empty stomach lurch crazily. "Why were you following us?"

Koos smiled, his pale eyes glittering in the dim light. "I saw you and Jan sneak out, lots of times," he said. "I figured you were up to something bad, and you were."

Pieter sighed, his breath coming out ragged and edgy. Could he trust Koos not to open his mouth?

Pieter sighed again. "Promise you won't tell."

"Oh, I won't. I won't ever tell."

"Jan and I decided to start smoking."

"Yeah?" Now Koos was twitchy with excitement. "And you got those stubs down there by the track, so you don't have to buy them yourself. That's smart."

"There aren't any cigarettes to buy except on the black market, Koos," Jan said.

Don't let him think of any other reason to have cigarette butts, Pieter prayed. Don't let him make that connection.

"Is it fun?" Koos smiled, his face rounding into the shape of a cabbage. "Can I do it sometime?"

"Sure, sometime. Now let's go home." Pieter followed him wearily, suddenly drained and exhausted. Now he had one more worry. Koos, and what he might say and to whom. But right now, all he wanted was to go home and pull his bedcovers over his head.

Koos paused at the edge of the field. "Are you going home?" he asked.

"Yes, it's late," Pieter said. "And we're not supposed to be out here, remember? Do you want me to walk with you?"

"No." Koos sounded insulted. "I got out here by myself, so I can get home by myself. I know the way."

"Sorry," Pieter whispered. "I'm glad you're not afraid of the dark anymore, Koos. That's good." And he'd come alone. That was even better.

Koos turned onto the dirt road that bordered the field, then headed for the center of the village, where he lived with his parents in rooms above the family's tavern.

Pieter watched until his cousin's round figure disappeared into the ground fog. For a moment he was tempted to follow him, then decided against it. Koos would be all right. Even if the night patrol found him out after curfew, they'd dismiss him as that dull-witted kid of the tavern keeper's. Even the Moffen tolerated Koos.

"See you tomorrow," Jan said, and disappeared into the fog.

Pieter waited until a cloud blanketed the quarter moon before hurrying across the road and into the shelter of a hawthorn hedge. A moment later he slipped through the narrow hole he'd cut in the bushes. Quickly he ran through the tangled lot on the other side before coming to his own backyard. Now he could see his two-story brick house clearly, and he stopped to watch and wait.

The waiting began again. He forced himself to do it. Watch and wait, make sure all is well. If anything is out of place, even a leaf on a tree, watch and wait some more. He hated it. The fear began to fill him again, and he felt powerless against it.

Their blackout curtains were closed, but Pieter could detect a glow of palest candlelight coming from the kitchen window. Mama must be sitting there, waiting for him. That was normal — in fact, everything seemed in order. It was all right to go in. This time.

He hurried across the shabby backyard, covered with brittle leaves from the lone elm, to the back door of the kitchen. The tree was the last one standing; the rest had gone to firewood. After this winter, their yard would be treeless.

When he opened the door, the odor of cooked tulip bulbs filled the room and made him gag. For a moment he thought he would vomit.

"Oh, Pieter, at last." He could see Mama sitting at the table, hunched over the stub of candle, hands outstretched to its warmth. "I've been so worried. Do you want some supper?"

He thought of the bulbs and quickly answered no. "Mama, you should be in bed. At least you'd be warmer." People used to say he'd inherited his mother's looks: thick, dark-blonde hair, deep blue eyes, and a sprinkling of freckles across an upturned nose. Since the war began, though, Mama had faded, like an old snapshot. Her hair, her skin, even her eyes had dimmed to a dull gray.

She looked at him intently now. "I couldn't sleep, not until I talked to you."

When he heard the quiver in her voice, Pieter was instantly alert. His body filled with tension again. He ached with it, hated it. Fear crept along his backbone and turned it to mush. "What? Tell me." He sat down heavily across from her.

"Beppie van Dijk — you know, the girl from church — came here tonight. She was astonished that I didn't know you were delivering the underground news sheets for Free Holland."

Pieter felt himself collapsing inside. He didn't want Mama to know. She couldn't handle it.

"What you are doing is too dangerous." Mama's voice was thick with her own fear. "More dangerous than the bent smokes, even. You must stop, Pieter. I can't lose you to the war, too."

"You won't lose me, Mama. I promise." But his promises were beginning to sound the same. Hollow, with no ring of belief in them. He tried to sit up straight and look as if he could take on the world. But inside he was weak with the knowledge that this might be the one promise he couldn't keep.

CHAPTER 3

The Message

Sunday, September 17

Pieter saw Beppie in church the next afternoon. Outside, the day felt sunny and warm, but inside, damp, cold air remained trapped between the stone walls. Without fuel for the furnace, the church soon would feel like the middle of an iceberg. During the harshest months of winter, only the most religious members attended. Pieter wasn't one of them. He came to church to make Mama happy. It also gave him another chance to look at Beppie. Just staring at her shimmering blonde hair sent mysterious tinglings throughout his body.

She sat several pews ahead, between her parents, her back as straight as a tulip stem. She must be fifteen now, an older woman by two years, and looking it too. She was thin, but that only made the soft places on her body more fascinating to stare at. Even wearing a faded green dress and an old mended sweater, she looked like one of the Royals to him. Although the Queen and her daughters had been in exile since the Germans came, he still remembered their fairy-tale looks.

Pastor Kooiman stood now and walked to the altar while the organist forced out an introduction to the first hymn. Pieter was waiting for the day when the organ would finally collapse in a heap of groans and wheezes. It would be one casualty of the war he wouldn't mind. Everyone began to sing now, and Pieter, after a poke from Mama, mouthed the words. But his head was still full of delicious thoughts of Beppie and what she had wanted to tell him last night.

Kazan. Had she seen him? No, she wouldn't risk curfew over a dog. Then did she know something about the train and why it changed schedules to stop and wait as it did? Suddenly Beppie turned and looked directly at him, those dark blue eyes warming him under his thin Sunday pants and jacket. He wanted her look to be personal, but he knew it was a signal to meet him after services. It was the courier business, nothing more.

But what business? Now, as Pastor Kooiman began his sermon, Pieter wondered if he'd last until he knew. Suddenly his clothes felt tighter, his arms began to itch, and he had a tickling urge to cough.

Jan and his parents hurried in and found places two rows ahead, in front of Mr. van der Meer, their teacher. What had made Mr. and Mrs. de Waard late? Pieter wondered. Papa had said they were always so punctual that the village didn't need a clock in the square. It could use the de Waards to tell time.

An hour later, Pastor Kooiman began to wind down, asking everyone to pray for what was uppermost in their hearts. Pieter immediately began praying for shorter sermons, then quickly stopped as the overhead lights flickered several times. He wondered if that was a sign from God that He was upset. Pieter decided to show a little more respect. During a war, he couldn't be too careful.

Pastor Kooiman paused now as the lights flickered out completely. Was he also thinking it was a message from heaven? Pieter raised his head and looked around. Jan was looking too, and so were Beppie and several others. Maybe the electric lights were going the way of the organ.

Mama pushed his head down again so that he could see nothing but the tops of his worn, scuffed shoes. Then he heard the wave of sound, a whispering coming directly toward him, down their pew.

"They've landed at Oosterbeek," someone whispered. "Pass it on."

Oosterbeek? It was no more than sixty kilometers away. But who had landed? The Brits? The Yanks?

Mama plucked at Pieter's sleeve as they all stood for the final blessing. "What did the message mean?" Her eyes shone with emotion.

"I'll find out." Pieter began to thread his way through the knots of people gathering in the aisle. Koos grabbed his jacket, but Pieter shrugged him off. No time for Koos just now.

He bolted outside to look for Beppie and saw her green dress disappearing around a corner of the church.

16

She was headed for their special meeting place, the old storage shed in back.

He followed her and stepped inside. "Beppie," he whispered as his eyes adjusted to the dimness. Slowly the outlines of broken gravestones from the cemetery began to take shape in the dusky light.

"Here," she whispered back.

He felt his way across the windowless room until he could hear her breathing and smell her freshness. How could she smell so clean when there was practically no soap to be had in all of The Netherlands?

"What happened at Oosterbeek?" he blurted out. "Do you know?"

"First things first. Where were you last night?" she demanded. "You should have been home much earlier."

"Someone followed Jan and me to the bent smokes, and I had to see who it was." Pieter leaned against a gravestone and sighed. "It was only Koos."

"*Only* Koos?" Beppie's voice took on a harshness. "He can be as dangerous as anyone else."

"I know." Why couldn't she be friendlier? If only she'd notice him as a person, as almost a man.

"I came to your house to tell you that from now on, you have to spend more time as a courier."

"Because of Oosterbeek?" Now Pieter forgot his personal feelings. "What happened? What's it got to do with the news sheets?"

"Slow down," Beppie said. "After today, you won't be delivering the news sheets. Someone else will take your place. British paratroopers landed at Oosterbeek this morning, and many of the Resistance fighters have come out of hiding to help them. They're going to need ration cards for identification, or the Moffen will pick them up easily at checkpoints."

She knew last night, he thought. She knew about the paratroopers before they landed.

"But what does all this have to do with me?" He tried to sound calm, but inside, his heart was pounding crazily, as if it were trying to get away.

"The cards have to be delivered to the next courier, and right now there's no one else available to do it." Beppie paused, then added, "They're counterfeit cards, of course."

Counterfeit. What else did he expect? But this only made it worse. "But I can't . . ."

"Yes, you can," Beppie interrupted. "I'll give you the directions. It's almost the same as delivering the news sheets."

No, it isn't, he wanted to say. It's more dangerous, worse than the news sheets. Running counterfeit ration cards: people had been dragged off to prison for this, shot — not just grown-ups but kids like him.

"You're not scared, are you?" Beppie's voice sounded as if such a thing had never entered her mind. To be scared. She looked soft, but she must be made of steel and granite, nothing but hard stuff inside.

"No, I'm not scared," he answered. Another lie, like the time he delivered news sheets and told Mama he was at Jan's house, studying. But he couldn't admit how he felt. This was no time to be frightened. The

Resistance needed him now, more than ever. "Is this the beginning of the liberation? Will we be free soon?"

"I don't know." Beppie sounded tired. "But it can't be too much longer."

"I'll do it," Pieter said, as if it had ever been a question.

"Good." Beppie nodded. "Oh, I forgot. When you make the delivery next Wednesday, you'll have to be dressed like a girl. But don't worry. I'll lend you some of my clothes."

Then she opened the door and was gone.

CHAPTER 4

More Problems

Monday, September 18

In class the next morning, Pieter tried hard to concentrate on his book, but history was nothing more than a boring jumble of dates. Especially now, since the Moffen had rearranged everything. At the beginning of the war, they had taken away the books, then returned them with pages missing. But the Nazis weren't fooling anyone. The missing pages must say something bad about them and something good about the Jews. After the war, Pieter vowed, he would find out.

Thoughts of his courier job on Wednesday flooded his mind again. He couldn't stop thinking about it. The fear, the tension as he waited kept him awake at night, made him break out in sweats. How many hours left? Forty-eight. Forty-eight hours until his last bicycle ride. After the war, the villagers would erect a plaque in the square that read, "Pieter van Dirk, 1931-1944, brave, unafraid, gallant warrior of the Resistance." Beppie would bring her children and grandchildren to see the plaque, medals gleaming on her soft, round chest, tears glistening in her blue eyes as she spoke of their love.

"Pieter. Pieter van Dirk."

Everyone in the room began to snicker as Pieter finally realized that Mr. van der Meer had called on him. But what had he said?

"Sir? I didn't hear. It's my ears — I have a cold." Pieter tried hard to sound as if he had a terrible infection.

But the look in Mr. van der Meer's cold-potato eyes said he didn't believe that for a second. "I hope you'll be able to hear better when the lunch bell rings." He gave Pieter a thin smile. "We wouldn't want you to miss lunch."

He walked to his desk and picked up a book. "Meanwhile, turn to your literature books. Today we will begin to read the works of the German writers from the lower Ruhr Valley. Although we have Dutch translations, they are much more beautiful to read in the original German. Just listen to this."

Then he began to read lines of German words that made no sense to Pieter. What did he care about a bunch of Germans sitting around, writing poems about a valley that now brought misery to everyone with the manufacture of bombs and bullets? He tried to stifle a yawn, but was too late.

"Well, Pieter, I see you are bored by these poems," Mr. van der Meer said. "Do you know how long I went to the university in Munich to study this literature in its original German?"

21

"No, sir," Pieter said. How many times had they heard this story about studying in Germany?

"Perhaps you'd rather I quoted one of the mindless songs the Allies play on their shortwave? How about 'G.I. Jive' or 'Boogie Woogie Bugle Boy'? Would that be better?"

"No, sir." Why was he listening to shortwave? Pieter wondered. That was not allowed unless . . . unless he had special permission.

Pieter was the first one out the door at noon. He wouldn't see Beppie because she was in high school, but he and Jan could talk about Oosterbeek. And he wouldn't have to endure Mr. van der Meer's stares until lunch was over.

"Pieter, wait." Jan hurried toward him, lanky and loose-limbed, his hair a dark clump of curls in need of a brush. Together the two walked across the playground to its sunnier side. "What did Beppie tell you at church yesterday?"

Pieter bit into his carrot sandwich so he'd have time to think about his answer. How did Jan know about his meetings with Beppie? Jan had been his shadow since kindergarten. He knew everything Pieter was thinking. Except, this was different, private.

"She . . . she talked about Oosterbeek," Pieter began. That was safe. Everyone was talking about it.

"Well, what did she say?" Jan was bursting with excitement.

"Here comes Koos," Pieter said. "We'll talk later."

Koos walked up, a big grin splitting his face in

22

half. "I know what you and that girl did in the shed together yesterday," he said.

Pieter looked at Jan and raised one eyebrow. Did the entire world know about his secret meetings with Beppie? "What girl?"

"That real pretty one." Koos pulled an apple out of his lunch sack and bit noisily into it.

"What did we do?" Pieter asked angrily. "What?" Koos was getting to be a real pest.

"You kiss and hug, that's what." Koos laughed so hard that bits of apple flew from his mouth.

Pieter felt his face flame. He couldn't stop it.

"You ought to see your face." Koos laughed harder. "It's the color of a beet."

Even Jan was having trouble not smiling. Pieter pounded off with Jan right behind him, and Koos flying after the two of them. "Hey, I was supposed to tell you to come over after school. We've got extra food this time."

Pieter forced himself to simmer down at the mention of extra food. "Thanks, Koos. I'll be there."

Jan waited until Koos wandered off before he spoke. "They don't miss a meal at his house, do they?" He sounded angry, and he pushed his dark, curly hair away from his face in a furious gesture.

"Uncle Bro gets to keep a bigger quota of food because of the tavern, that's all."

"So he can feed the German soldiers who come there." Jan kicked viciously at a pebble.

Pieter knew there was more to Jan's anger than just the food. It was the other thought that swam to

23

the top of his mind too, and bobbed there, like something dead. Did Uncle Bro feed those Nazis more than food in the tavern? Information, maybe? That thought stayed with him the rest of the afternoon.

After school, Pieter got on his bicycle, its bare wheels making rasping sounds on the cobblestone street. Rubber tires had disappeared when the Germans arrived. The Moffen had taken them all. He pedaled quickly on the road that bordered the canal for half a kilometer before he crossed the bridge leading to the village center. Uncle Bro's tavern sat on the busiest corner in town, with the bridge and canal on one side and the road leading to Overloon on the other. No German cars or trucks polluted the parking spaces in front of the tavern today, though. Good.

As he stepped indoors, Pieter sniffed the smoky remains of last night's fire in the hearth and the acidy scent that lingered from the acorn coffee Aunt Gerda brewed for customers.

More and more, the old times leaped to Pieter's mind when he came here. In the winter, after skimming on skates for hours on the frozen canals, families gathered inside the tavern for singing and talking around the open brick hearth. Even Kazan came in and snoozed in a contented ball before the fire.

All the children drank Uncle Bro's rich, steaming chocolate while the grown-ups chatted over their beer. Sometimes, if his parents lingered too long and Pieter grew sleepy, his father carried him home through a starry night that squeaked with cold.

Now Pieter paused in the dimness of the tavern,

noticing that the ceiling, with its smoky rafter beams, seemed lower each time he came. Sometime soon he might have to duck through the short doorway as he entered, just as his father and brothers did.

Uncle Bro appeared in the doorway that separated the public room from the stairway to the family quarters. He always looked as if he'd just enjoyed a good meal. Nicely rounded, Uncle Bro appeared soft and flabby. But Pieter knew that muscles and temper rippled under the softness that he displayed to the world.

"Pieter," he boomed in a voice that filled the tavern. "Koos said you might be coming." He walked to the bar on the other side of the room and produced two large turnips and three small potatoes from a shelf underneath. "Your mama can work her magic on these."

"Thank you, Uncle Bro." Pieter put the vegetables in his tattered book bag, then looked around at the empty room. "No customers yet. Have the Moffen started to pull out?"

Uncle Bro shook his head. "We must not begin to mistake the Nazis for tourists. The war is not over just because the Allies sent a few paratroopers."

Two elderly men clattered in on their worn *klompen* and began to talk excitedly. Mr. de Waard had followed them in and sliced the air with his huge hands as he made a point. Would Jan be as big as his father one day, Pieter wondered, and have a complexion that always looked sunburned?

Suddenly there was an explosion of laughter, and

the men began to pound one another on the back. "Oosterbeek is only the beginning," one of them shouted. "Soon the Moffen will be eating dog meat!"

Dog meat? He didn't mean that.

Pieter grabbed his book bag and ran outside. Kazan was still alive, and so were his father and brothers. Pieter had to believe that, no matter what anyone said.

A piece of paper was tacked to the front door that hadn't been there when he came in a few minutes ago. One look, and he knew exactly what it was. Another list of Resistance fighters caught and taken away by the Nazis. They posted the lists to frighten everyone, and it worked. Each time Pieter saw a list, he stopped breathing as he looked for his brothers' names.

He didn't find them, not this time. Slowly he drew in a deep breath, relieved for one short moment. Then another thought chilled him. After Wednesday, would his own name be posted there?

CHAPTER 5

A Secret Errand

Wednesday, September 20

Pieter awakened early on Wednesday morning, instantly alert. What was it? he wondered, sitting up straight in bed and listening. A noise, different sounding, outside, but not far. He shivered, colder than he'd ever been.

Now the faint rumble became louder, low and steady, as it headed toward the village. He'd heard it before in some long-ago time when he was younger. But then his father had been here and his brothers too, and their presence had given him a feeling of protection. Now he had no feeling of that at all.

He got up, tiptoed to the window, and opened it. The rumbling grew louder. Motors, engines of some kind, growling and clanking along, and the sound of metal grating on the road.

He grabbed his father's old robe, shrugged it on, and opened his bedroom door. The house was still as he hurried downstairs.

"Pieter." Mama's voice drifted toward him like smoke out of the near-dawn darkness. "Don't go outside." She stood near the front window as she spoke.

"I've got to see what it is." He dashed out and stopped on the cobblestone walk. Neighbors were coming out of their houses too, looking sleepy and afraid in their nightclothes.

Mr. de Jong, the elderly man next door, opened his door and peered out. "Pieter, is that you?" He blinked rapidly.

Pieter walked over to his yard. "Yes, sir. Do you know what's making that noise? I think I've heard it before."

Mr. de Jong came outside now, his faded bathrobe tied together with a piece of string. "Tanks," he said shortly. "I'll never forget that sound. When the Moffen came in 1940, that noise started after the airplanes stopped. I'll never forget it, never." He spat on the sidewalk as if to rid himself of the remembrance.

Four years ago last May. Pieter hadn't been paying much attention to things then. But he did remember that terrifying sound, and he'd been afraid ever since. The fear had begun then, seeping through everything, like the sea through a crack in a dike.

"Where are they going?" Pieter asked. "There's nothing left in that direction for the Nazis to take."

"They're headed for Overloon," Mr. de Jong said. "That's all there is south of here for them to worry about."

Overloon. Pieter was going near there this afternoon for Beppie and the Resistance. Something cold grabbed his heart, then spread through his veins to the rest of his body until he felt frozen inside. Fear, the numbing fear — it was always that.

"Something is going on. Something is about to happen there," Mr. de Jong went on.

"It's so near," Pieter whispered.

"As near as our firesides, that's how near the war is." Mr. de Jong pulled his robe tighter about him. "Pray that we survive it." After one more glance down the road, the old man went back inside his house and slammed the door.

Pieter hurried inside his house too, glad that Mama hadn't heard Mr. de Jong. He found her in the kitchen, slicing two pieces of bread from the loaf they'd bartered for with the tobacco. With a sigh, he realized he'd have to go for more bent smokes again, and soon. Now, though, he had to tell Mama another lie.

"Beppie has invited me to her house to do my homework today."

It was a lie as flimsy as the lace curtains that hung in their windows, mended so many times that there was nothing left of them but the patches.

Mama wasn't fooled. "Not the news sheets again. Please, Pieter, don't."

"No, it isn't the news sheets." That much was true anyway. "And I won't be late. Don't worry."

Later that afternoon, Pieter stood in Beppie's spare bedroom, wearing her faded green dress, her sweater, and a pair of her socks and shoes, wondering if he could go through with it.

29

As he tied her scarf over his head, he looked closely in the dusty mirror above the dresser. Was that a bit of fuzz on his upper lip? Maybe a sign of whiskers? If he was stopped by a patrol, they would detect it immediately.

"You don't look like a real girl," he told his image. "You'll never get away with it." He walked downstairs to the parlor where Beppie was waiting.

"Perfect but for one thing," she said, after scrutinizing his disguise. Then she picked up a pair of scissors lying on the hall table and cut a piece of curly blonde hair from each side of her own face.

"What are you doing?" he shouted.

Quickly she came to stand before him and tucked one piece of hair over each ear, leaving the short ends to show outside the scarf.

"Now you look just like me," she said. Then she picked up a knitting bag with needles sticking out of the top and handed it to him. "There are more than one hundred ration cards inside," she went on. "Deliver these to the red farmhouse on the corner of Polder Road and the Venray turnoff, ten kilometers directly south of here. The name on the mailbox is van Hal, and if anyone asks you where you're going, say, 'I'm going to visit Granny.'"

"That's all I say?"

"Yes. The Germans think that's where my grandmother lives, and I go to visit her each Wednesday afternoon. They have seen me so many times they don't even stop me anymore. Of course, now, with things the way they are . . ."

30

She didn't finish, and it didn't matter. After this morning, he knew how things were. More dangerous than ever before.

"Who really lives there, Beppie?"

"A brave member of the Resistance. One of the bravest."

At last he would meet a real hero. "Why aren't you going today?"

Her soft, pretty face suddenly closed, as if a book had been shut on a story before it ended. "If you don't know, you can't tell. Now go, or it will be dark before you get back. And take my bicycle, of course. Leave yours in the garden shed."

He hurried outside, Beppie's shoes pinching his feet. Good thing he didn't have to walk. As it was, he'd have blisters before he got home tonight. If he'd still be alive to feel them.

He began to pedal south out of town, the bicycle's wheel rims scraping against the road. The dress caught on his knees and he pulled it higher, to make better time.

After an hour's steady riding through rolling meadows and sandy ridges, Pieter neared the Venray turnoff. He hadn't seen a Moffen tank or a single Moffen soldier. Where had they gone since this morning? Their absence was nearly as threatening as their presence. Maybe he'd walk into a trap at the farmhouse. Maybe they were waiting for him there.

Now the red house stood before him, and he dropped the bicycle on the gravelly path before it. He slowly walked up the porch steps, then knocked on the door. It opened quickly, as if someone had watched him approach. Of course the Moffen would be watching for him, he thought in a flash of panic. Now he couldn't possibly get away.

A boy, tired-looking and dirty, and not much older than he, stared at him without speaking. Naturally they'd have a boy at the front door. Boys trusted other boys, didn't they?

Suddenly Pieter realized he should say something. So he'd say what was expected. "I came to visit Granny." His voice shook, sounding like neither boy nor girl.

"Come," was all the boy said, then stood aside so Pieter could enter. He glanced around at the shabby furnishings, dusty and fading with age. The only sound came from a grandfather clock, tick-tocking in a corner. Otherwise, the quiet was deathlike.

"This way," the boy gestured, and led him down a short hall to a door at the end. The boy knocked, then said, "The delivery has come."

"Enter."

Pieter drew in a deep breath and slowly opened the door. The room was dark, gloomy; heavy drapes were pulled over the window. He couldn't see and knew it was a trap for sure now. The Germans had taken away the real heroes. He knew that as much as he knew he was breathing. Across the room he saw a dark figure seated in a straight-backed chair. Now the figure beckoned to him, and Pieter walked unsteadily across the room toward it. "I've been expecting you," a woman said.

CHAPTER 6

Confrontation

A moment later

Pieter gulped in a breath of air. He must have made a choking sound because the person in the chair said, "Don't be afraid. I'm only your old granny."

Pieter took another step closer. Now he could see that an elderly, frail-looking woman sat there. So quiet, so ordinary. It had to be a trap. How could she be a hero of the Resistance?

"My name is Auntie Riek," she said softly. But there was a command in her voice as she continued, "Now give me the knitting bag. Quickly."

She knew all about the ration cards, then. But that didn't mean anything. The Moffen had a way of coaxing people to tell. Pieter didn't hesitate, just handed over the knitting bag, eager to be finished with his mission and gone. He watched as she looked inside.

"Good," she murmured. "Good."

"May I go now?" Pieter whispered, surprised he'd managed to speak at all.

"Go into the other room and wait one hour," she said. "Then you may leave."

"Why must I wait?" he whispered. Why did he have to wait even another minute?

"You always visit your granny for one hour," she said. "We must not change anything, not anything, you understand? The boy, Henk, will tell you when to leave."

So that was it, he thought as he returned to the dark, dusty parlor. They were sending for the Moffen, and it would take one hour for them to get here and take him away.

But no one came while Pieter waited the longest hour of his life. Finally Henk appeared.

They're letting me go, Pieter realized. No Moffen. No arrest. We're all on the same side. Henk, Auntie Riek, and I are all good guys. "It's time to leave," he said.

Outside, Pieter picked up Beppie's bicycle and began to pedal hard, hiking up the dress so that he could go even faster. The road began to show signs of life now. Dutch bicyclists pedaled by on creaking wheels; occasionally a German truck passed. Once a Nazi soldier waved to him, and Pieter worried about it until he remembered. He was dressed as a girl, and the soldier was flirting with him.

Pieter was grateful for the gathering dusk, glad no one could see his face clearly. He kept his head lowered and pedaled faster, thinking of nothing else but home and safety. But that was a joke. No one was safe anywhere. Hadn't the Moffen taken Papa from his bed in the middle of the night?

A light drizzle had begun earlier. Now, as he rode into his village, the drizzle increased to rain. Darkness hovered, and curfew would begin soon. But all he needed was a few more minutes and he'd be home and out of this silly dress.

Suddenly he heard someone pedaling up behind him, coming fast. Had he been followed? He should have been more careful, should have watched. Maybe it was Koos. At least he would be a familiar face.

"Pieter, is that you?"

He nearly fell off his bicycle as he looked around. "Jan?" he whispered. "How did you recognize me?"

"I'd know your skinny legs anywhere," Jan said, pulling up beside him. "But why are you in that getup, and why are you riding Beppie's bike?" Pieter thought he heard a snicker in Jan's voice. "Come to think of it, you look pretty cute."

"Shut up." Pieter could feel his face burn. He knew that Jan was teasing, but still, it was hard to take.

"Now I know." Jan paused as two elderly women pedaled slowly past. "You've been on an errand for Beppie."

"How did you figure it out?" Pieter blurted out.

"Her dress and her bike," Jan said. "Easy." His quick grin was reassurance.

"Promise you won't mention this to anyone, hear?" Pieter already knew Jan would never give up his friend's secrets, not intentionally. But someone in the village had informed on his father, even on Kazan. Kazan. How he longed for his dog, yearned to hide his face in the thick fur the way he did when he was little and afraid. He was so tired of being afraid.

"Oh, oh," Jan whispered. "Moffen ahead." Pieter looked up to see two German soldiers who had suddenly appeared at the end of the block. They glanced at Pieter and Jan, seemingly without interest, and continued to walk and talk. But suddenly they stopped in the middle of the street, hunching their jacket collars higher as the rain increased.

Pieter immediately began to think about ways to escape. Uncle Bro's tavern was less than a block away. Maybe he and Jan could sneak in the back door and wait until the soldiers went somewhere else. Maybe —

"You two, wait right there." One of the soldiers hurried toward them.

"You do the talking, Jan," Pieter whispered. "I don't sound like a girl." He didn't think he could talk anyway. He felt as if words would choke in his throat.

Both soldiers stood before them now. "Whose cycles are these?" the taller of the two demanded in poor Dutch.

Pieter lowered his head after taking a quick glance at them. The shorter one looked no older than his brother Menno, who was barely seventeen. His blond mustache was only a token, and his cheeks bore scars of pimples.

"These bicycles belong to us," Jan said. "They are very old, no tires."

"I can see that." The taller soldier spoke again. "But they will have to do, since we have nothing else. I am tired of walking patrol in the rain."

"But we need them for school," Jan objected.

The taller soldier grabbed Jan's bicycle and pushed it back and forth. "We shall have to requisition tires," he went on as if Jan hadn't spoken.

"Good luck." Jan's anger was clear in his voice. "There's not a tire to be found in the Netherlands. You have sent them all to Germany."

Pieter wanted to run, but he dared not move. This time Jan had gone too far. If he made the soldiers angry enough, who knows what they might do? Why couldn't Jan be quiet? Once, in third grade, Jan's temper got them in trouble at church when he —

"Come, darling, let us have your bicycle too," the other soldier said.

Jan gave Pieter a poke. The soldier was talking to him! He pushed the bicycle forward and tried to draw back. How would he explain to Beppie that he'd let a German take her bicycle?

"Not so fast, darling. Maybe we'll take you along with the bicycle." The soldier put his hand on Pieter's.

"Leave her alone." Suddenly Jan was beside him, his arm around Pieter's waist. "She's my girl."

The soldiers began to laugh. "Well, what have we here?" the shorter one said. "The big protector of Dutch womanhood." He pinched Pieter's shoulder, then took the bicycle.

"She's too skinny for you, Gottfried," the taller soldier said impatiently. "Come on, let's go."

Pieter couldn't wait to wash his hand where the soldier had touched it. In fact, there wasn't enough soap in the world to make it feel clean.

"Are you all right?" Jan whispered as they watched the Germans wheel the bicycles across the street.

"I think so, but that was really close, Jan. Too close."

"I know." Jan breathed a huge sigh.

"Let's go to Uncle Bro's, use the back entrance. I need to wait until those Moffen go somewhere else before I go to Beppie's and change my clothes."

"Understood."

As Pieter continued to watch the soldiers, a sudden movement two doorways down caught his attention. Had he been followed after all? Or was he so jumpy that he was ready to leap out of his skin at every little thing?

"Jan, did you see . . ."

"Oh, oh," Jan whispered. Pieter turned to look in the same direction as Jan. Suddenly he felt surrounded by danger. "There's Koos, standing by the tavern door."

"But it's only Koos," Pieter said, then remembered Beppie's words. Koos could be as dangerous as anyone else.

"Better not let him see you dressed like that," Jan said.

"Right." Pieter slipped into a covered doorway, and Jan followed. Then they waited and watched Koos. Had he seen them?

Koos stared in their direction as if he were trying to decide his next move. Suddenly he hurried inside.

Someone was coming. Footsteps hurried along the cobblestone sidewalk on their side of the street. More soldiers? It must be curfew now, Pieter realized. They'd be picked up, and his identity would be revealed. How could he explain the dress?

"What a relief," Jan said. "It's only my father." He stepped out to greet him.

Yes, that much was a relief. But what about Koos? What had he seen? And who was across the street, watching them? In the palest glow of light left at dusk, Pieter could see the tips of a pair of black boots in the shadows of the doorway. Whoever belonged to them had been standing there for a while and didn't want to be seen . . . by anyone.

CHAPTER 7

Where's Beppie?

Moments later

Even after Jan hurried out of the doorway to walk with his father to the tavern, Pieter remained standing there, alone. He knew he had to move soon, but he felt trapped.

Finally he forced himself to take a quick look at the doorway down the block, to see if the person wearing the black boots was still there, waiting for him to make the first move. Pieter could see raindrops dripping from the roof above him, then the glistening wet stones of the street, and finally the doorway. But darkness had nearly capped a lid over everything, most of all the boots. The doorway appeared to be empty.

He'd have to risk it, and maybe it wasn't that great a risk now. Maybe he'd done something smart for once. After all, if he couldn't see across the street, neither could the wearer of the boots.

Pieter eased off Beppie's shoes so he'd make no

sound on the cobblestones and tucked her curls under the head scarf, pulling it closer to his face. Then he slipped from the doorway. If Beppie was back from her mysterious errand and found he hadn't returned, she'd be worried. But where had she gone?

Silently he padded down the street until he could cut through lanes behind houses. He paused once under an overhang only long enough to wipe rain from his face and glance behind him. No one was there. He hadn't realized he'd been holding his breath until he let it out in a long, whooshing sound. So far, so good. A deep quiet filled the darkness now as curfew brought Dutch life to a close for another day.

A small light shone dimly from Beppie's kitchen window. She must be there with her parents, having supper. He hated to think of what she was going to say when she found out about her bicycle. Her fury would light up the power plant.

Beppie's mother answered his knock on the back door.

"Yes?" She squinted into the darkness, then cried out as she saw Pieter in her daughter's clothes.

"It's only me," Pieter said. "Sorry if I startled you, Mrs. van Dijk."

She opened the door wide enough for him to enter. "I don't understand you young people. You're in Beppie's clothes, and she's wearing her brother's, gone off on some foolhardy errand. Oh, Pieter, what is the sense of it? Will it end the war any sooner?"

He began to shiver violently as he stood there, unable to answer. The idea of Beppie, probably riding

his bicycle, going off on an errand dressed as a boy —
it was overwhelming. It was almost too frightening to
think about.

But he couldn't get it out of his mind as he hurried
upstairs to change out of the sodden dress and sweater.
Why couldn't he have gone on that errand instead of
Beppie? Did she think he wasn't brave enough or smart
enough to do it? Surely she didn't think he was too
young.

Pieter stopped lacing his shoes for a moment
to consider. What explained Beppie's fierceness, her
blowtorch temper, her refusal to be afraid of anything?
Why did she act as if she had to win the war all by
herself?

When he finished putting on his own clothes, he
said goodnight to the van Dijks and left the house. He
glanced in the garden shed, but his bicycle wasn't there.
Not that he expected to find it. He could only wonder
and guess where Beppie and his bicycle were at that
moment. And worry. Worry and pray that she was all
right. Yes, pray. God really came in handy at times
like this.

Although Pieter arrived home reasonably early,
Mama was still tense and anxious.

"Oh, Pieter, you're home at last."

"I'm all right, Mama. You mustn't worry."

"But the Nazis. They're everywhere. You must be
careful."

How many times had she said that? he wondered.
How many times had he?

"Don't think of them, Mama. Think of what will

be when they're gone and Papa is home. And Menno and Gerrit and Kazan. Think of that."

"I'll try," she said. She came to him then and hugged him fiercely. Suddenly Pieter realized that he was now taller than she was. When had that happened? "Good night, Mama," he said, returning her hug.

After she took the candle stub and went upstairs to bed, he stood at the back door, listening. Satisfied that no one had followed him, he too went upstairs, but sleep was a long time coming.

Pieter waited for Beppie to contact him the next day and the day after that. When he didn't hear anything and, worse yet, didn't even see her going to and from school, he grew panicky. She seemed to have vanished. What had happened to her?

Finally, on Friday afternoon, he dared to walk past her house after school. He saw no one around, although he thought he saw the curtains move in the front window. But even that could have been his imagination. He wondered if he should look in the shed, to see if she'd brought his bicycle back. At least he'd know that she had been here. But after a few steps along the path while he considered, Pieter decided against it. Someone could be watching the house and would report anything out of order. He walked on, telling himself to stay calm, but that was like talking to the wind. It made no difference at all.

When Sunday finally came, Pieter hurried Mama to church early.

"What has come over you?" Mama whispered as

they sat in their pew listening to the squeaky organ prelude.

Pieter turned around, hoping to see Beppie. "It's warmer here than at home," he whispered back, then grinned at Jan as he wandered in behind his parents.

"Warmer?" Mama sounded disbelieving and pulled her old brown coat tighter to her. "By the way, what has happened to your bicycle? The truth this time. Remember, you're in church."

"Beppie needs it," he said, and he knew that for once he hadn't lied. Then he opened the Psalm book and began to study it with what he hoped looked like religious fervor. But he wasn't fooling anyone, probably not God and especially not Mama. He saw nothing on the pages but the lovely image of Beppie's beautiful face. Was that a dimple? No, only a speck of dirt on the page. He brushed it off and could almost imagine touching Beppie's soft skin.

The service began. Koos drifted in with his parents, and Mr. van der Meer seemed to glide in like an oily snake in a henhouse. Suddenly Pieter sat up straight. Was his teacher wearing black boots with pointed toes? Too late to see, because Mr. van der Meer had already sat down.

The service dragged on, and Pieter grew increasingly tense as he waited for Beppie. Her parents sat in their pew as usual. Dare he ask them about her? Finally he accepted that she wasn't going to appear, at least not today. The service was almost over. But what had happened to her? Oh, God, let her be all right. This is a real prayer this time — I really mean it. Give it your highest personal attention. If I'm being too personal, God, excuse me, but just this once, pay special attention to Beppie.

The moment Pastor Kooiman spoke the final "amen," Pieter dashed outside. Quickly, before anyone else came out, he ran back to the shed and flung open the door. He didn't care who saw him. But it was empty. Beppie wasn't there, hadn't been.

"Where'd you go?" Jan asked as Pieter returned to the churchyard moments later. People had come out now, to stand in small clusters and talk.

"Had to pee," Pieter answered. "Couldn't wait for the toilet inside."

"*Ja*, all those old ladies take so much time," Jan snickered. "Say, have you heard about the bridge at Arnhem? Pa got the news this morning."

"What news?" Pieter felt himself go rigid. Was that where Beppie had gone?

"There's a big fight going on for the bridge." Jan's voiced throbbed with excitement. "Guess the Resistance is in the thick of it, you know, helping the Allies and all."

First the paratroopers at Oosterbeek, and now this bridge at Arnhem. Of course Resistance fighters would be everywhere. That meant more ration cards would be needed. Surely Beppie would have to contact him soon. He'd better go home, and quickly.

Pieter looked around for Mama. Pastor Kooiman was speaking earnestly to her, touching her arm as he spoke. Probably telling her to pray harder. That was his answer to everything.

45

"I have to rescue Mama," Pieter told Jan, and threaded his way through the people toward her.

Suddenly someone grabbed his jacket sleeve and yanked hard. Pieter whirled around, irritated. "Koos, you want to tear the only jacket I own?"

"Wait till you hear." Koos breathed moistly, his eyes bright-blue specks in his round face. "Mr. van der Meer said I could go to camp."

"What camp?" Pieter looked around for the teacher. What business did he have getting Koos stirred up like this over something that could never happen?

"The camp for kids like me. You know, I take longer to learn."

Then Pieter saw Mr. van der Meer by the entrance to the cemetery, talking to several men. But he wore no pointed-toe black boots, just dirty old *klompen* like most men wore these days. It was all anyone had left.

Now Pieter saw Mama motioning to him. She was biting her lip and frowning. What had the pastor said to her? "Look, Koos, I have to go. We'll talk later."

"Tell Aunt Lida," Koos shouted after him. "Don't forget."

The moment Pieter reached his mother, she announced, "Pieter, we must go home quickly." Then she set off at a pace she hadn't used in years, at least not that Pieter had seen. Pieter jogged along to catch up.

Suddenly his heart lurched wildly inside him. Beppie! She'd heard something about Beppie! "Mama, is it . . ."

An elderly man wheeled his bicycle past them, and Mama began to speak pleasantly, as though she'd switched gears in her head. "I saw you talking to Koos. What did he say?" Her hands trembled as she fumbled with her coat buttons.

Pieter reported what his cousin had said.

Mama watched the old man until he was out of earshot. Then she turned to him. "Camp? Camp for a boy like Koos? Do you know what that is?" Bright circles of red appeared on Mama's pale cheeks. "It's a horrible place where the Moffen twist simple-minded children like him with their lies and turn them into little Nazi robots." She snapped off the final words before she marched on again. If she'd been carrying a gun on her shoulder, she couldn't have seemed more fierce than at that moment.

What had the pastor told her? It had changed his sweet mama into an angry tiger. It had to be about Beppie. Something terrible, something . . .

They stopped at the hedge near the border of their backyard. Usually Mama walked to the front door. But not today. She looked carefully behind them, then pushed through the hedge and walked quickly to the back door. Pieter felt as if his stomach had suddenly filled with stones. There was nothing left to do but follow her and hear the terrible news.

CHAPTER 8

A Mysterious Guest

A few minutes later

It was so quiet in the house that Pieter felt as if his heart had stopped. Even the blue clock on the mantel above the kitchen fireplace seemed to be holding its breath. But when Pieter stared at it, he could see the pendulum moving back and forth in the small curlicue opening beneath the face. It was two thirty-three. They'd never been home from church this early before.

At first glance, nothing seemed out of place. There were two potatoes in a pan on the stove, their skins scrubbed, waiting to be boiled. Now they ate the peelings, too. Sunday dinner.

Mama had already put out a dish of pickles on the table. They must be nearing the last of the jars she'd put up several years ago. Once he'd hated pickles. Now they were something else to eat.

Then he saw the hand towel on the rack above

the sink. It was neatly folded the way Mama always insisted on, but a corner of it hadn't come all the way down to meet the others. Underneath, Pieter could see spots of something dark. What was it? Dirt? No, something else . . .

Cold, numbing fear froze him to the spot where he stood. Who was in the house? "Mama." Pieter whispered the word, surprised to find he could speak at all. "Mama." He felt ashamed to be so afraid.

"Hush, Pieter," Mama whispered back. She turned, locked the kitchen door, then walked into the parlor. Pieter listened as her footsteps hurried quickly up the stairs and along the hall to his brothers' bedroom. Was Mama talking to someone?

In an instant it all became clear. Pieter raced up the stairs two at a time, skidding on the rag rug on the landing before he charged down the hall and took one step into the room. Mama was standing by the bed, staring down at someone lying there.

"Menno," Pieter whispered. "What has happened to him?"

Mama turned, tears running down her cheeks. "No, that isn't your brother in the bed. He's . . ." Her eyes focused behind Pieter.

Pieter whirled around. "Menno," he shouted, rushing to hug his brother, finding his once-chunky body now bone-sharp to touch. The wheat-colored beard and long, tangled hair made him seem old, a beginning-to-look-like-Papa old.

Then Pieter remembered the still form on the bed. "Who is that? Not . . ."

"No, it isn't Gerrit." Had Menno's voice always been so deep? "It's an American paratrooper."

"American?" Pieter rushed to the bed and looked down. He'd never seen an American in person before, and now here was one in his house. But something was wrong. Dark brown hair, matted with dirt, curled on the soldier's forehead. A shadow of beard, even darker than his hair, masked his thin, sweaty face. His eyes were closed, and he breathed heavily, as if a weight held down his chest.

"He's hurt, Menno," Pieter whispered. "Do something."

"I can't," Menno answered. "The minute I walk out on the street to get help, I'll be picked up."

"Is it bad?" Mama asked. "Maybe I can do something."

Menno opened the soldier's torn, dull-brown shirt partway, exposing a bandage caked with blood and dirt. It was patched over a discolored area on his shoulder. "He needs a doctor."

"I'll get Dr. Prager." Pieter started for the door.

"No!" Mama cried out. "There is a traitor among us in the village. It could be anyone, even Dr. Prager."

Menno sighed. "Yes, that's true. Perhaps we can get along without him. The bullet passed all the way through the American's shoulder. After the wound is cleaned and he's had a few days' rest, perhaps he will be all right."

"It's the best we can do." Mama brushed the soldier's hair away from his forehead. "He looks so young."

"Nineteen," Menno said. "He told me."

"Your brother's age." Mama touched his face once more.

The soldier's eyes snapped open, but he didn't appear to see them. He shuddered a deep breath and closed his eyes again.

"I'll get a clean bandage." Mama spoke quickly. "And boil some water. There may be something left in the medicine cabinet." She touched Menno tenderly before she left the room.

Pieter turned to follow his mother. "I'll help her." He had to get out of the room, quickly. Every emotion he'd ever known now seemed ready to well up and spill over. Especially his feelings for his family, yet he couldn't let his brother see him cry.

"Wait, Pieter," Menno said. He was smiling as Pieter slowly turned around. "Just look at you. So tall for a twelve-year-old."

"Thirteen. I've had a birthday while you've been away."

Menno touched his shoulder lightly. "Sorry I didn't get you a present. Next year. But now, I have to leave."

"No, you mustn't. You can't go yet." Pieter wanted to ask Menno if he'd seen Beppie, but he felt suddenly shy. Then his brother would know how he felt about her.

"I've been here too long, and someone is waiting to take me out of the village so I won't be seen. Take care of Mama, Pieter." Menno moved toward the door.

"But I have so many questions. About Gerrit and . . ."

51

"After the war, Pieter, I'll tell you everything. Gerrit's well — don't worry. And I'm sure Papa is, too. Good-bye, little brother."

Pieter listened to Mama crying downstairs as she said good-bye to Menno. Then the back door closed softly, and he knew his brother was gone. But how? Where? He rushed to the window, but there was no movement, no sound in the backyard below. Moments later, he heard the clip-clop of a horse and the creak of a wagon moving on the road beyond the hawthorn hedge.

"Farmer's wagon."

The words were so soft that Pieter wasn't sure he had heard them. Was he dreaming? He turned from the window. "Did you say something?"

"Farmer's wagon." Yes, it was the soldier's voice, barely a whisper. Now he opened his eyes. "Your brother . . . risked life . . . bring me." His voice was raspy-thin. "Farmer, too. Now you and your mother . . ." He faded into unconsciousness once more.

Heart pounding, head spinning, Pieter rushed downstairs. The soldier had spoken to him! In the kitchen, the copper teakettle was hissing with steam. Mama stood at the table, ripping an embroidered tablecloth into strips.

"I told myself that I wouldn't use this cloth again until your papa came home," Mama began. "But I don't think he'd mind if I used it now, for this."

"He spoke," Pieter said quickly. "The soldier spoke to me."

Mama stared at him. "How is that possible? You are suddenly a man of the world who understands English?"

"No!" Pieter cried out. "He spoke to me in Dutch! Not with an accent, either, like the Moffen. It was good, fine Dutch."

Pieter pounded back up the stairs, with Mama hurrying behind him. He rushed to the bed and bent down, pulling open the mud-caked shirt even further. Now the soldier's identification tags were visible on his thin, sweating chest. Carefully, Pieter turned them over. Yes, they carried American insignia marks, but the name definitely sounded Dutch. Jacob Baron. Underneath it was his identification number, his blood type, and the letter "J."

"He's American, but with a Dutch name," Pieter whispered.

Mama bent low. "Yes, I see. Look, there is something else on the chain, underneath the tags."

They recognized it at the same moment. They looked into each other's eyes and knew what it meant for the soldier . . . and for them.

"Dear God," Mama whispered. "It's the Star of David. He's a Jew."

CHAPTER 9

The Ghost Brigade

Later Sunday night

Pieter slipped out of the house as soon as it was dark. He crossed the backyard, pushed through the hedge, then hurried across the road. The tall grass swallowed him as he moved quietly through it toward the railroad tracks.

He couldn't let Jan know that he was going for more bent smokes tonight. There wasn't time, but more important, Jan couldn't know about their sudden need for more food. Then Jan would be in danger, too, and Pieter needed to watch out for his friend's safety as well. He could tell no one but Beppie about the wounded soldier, Jacob, lying now in Menno's bed. If Beppie ever came back. But she had to. He couldn't go through the rest of the war without her. Or worse, the rest of his life.

He crouched in the crumpled grass beside the tracks and began to wait. The grass had a rounded-out look here, as if an animal, maybe a dog, had slept in this place. Kazan. Where was he right now? On duty, guarding Moffen soldiers? Or maybe, just maybe, he was keeping a Nazi kitchen free of rats. He loved to kill rats. Miss a few, please, Kazan. Let the Nazis eat some rat dung.

Dampness seeped through Pieter's thin, worn pants. He began to shiver and pulled his jacket collar tighter to him. Where was that train? The bombing to the north would slow almost everything. But it was so hard to know what was really happening without a newspaper that didn't print lies and a radio that didn't shout propaganda. Real news came only from a friend's mouth.

Then he heard it: the familiar clickety-clack of wheels on rails. But the engine seemed to strain tonight, pulling its load more slowly. Finally the brakes grabbed the tracks, and the train ground to a halt at its usual place.

Pieter glanced through the whiskery tips of grass and choked off a gasp. The train was so long, longer than he'd ever seen it. Its last few cars simply disappeared into the ground mist. Doors squeaked open down the length of the train now, and heavy boots crunched on gravel as the low, guttural sounds of German came to him. What were the Moffen saying? Suddenly he regretted his refusal to learn even a few words.

Cigarette smoke drifted slowly to him, and another quick peek showed many more soldiers than usual milling about. That was good. He'd find enough bent smokes tonight to feed the extra mouth they had at home now.

Two soldiers strolled closer, stomping their feet to keep warm. One stopped, struck a match on his boot, and lit the cigarette already in his mouth. In that brief flash of light, Pieter saw the numbers 107 on the other soldier's shoulder patch and something printed directly beneath it.

Then Pieter heard another sound, faint, but totally recognizable. For an instant he was flooded with the warmth of remembering. There it was again. A dog's whine, a pleading to be set free. It came from the train, and that could only mean the soldiers had guard dogs with them. But what were they guarding?

Now the soldiers moved back to the train and clambered on. Doors closed, the train coughed, then began to chug down the tracks. It ran in total darkness. Not even a pale light glowed beneath its blackout shroud.

As soon as the train was out of sight, Pieter stood up and hurried to gather the bent smokes. He needed to get home with the tobacco, then see if Beppie had returned, so that he could tell her his news. If she wasn't home, he might have to take action on his own. The thought excited him as well as frightened him, and drove his heart into double time. Finished filling his sock at last, Pieter pushed through the tall grass, making too much noise and ignoring the caution warnings going off in his head.

Hurrying to the edge of the grass where it met the road, Pieter slipped on its dampness and fell, dropping the sock. Furiously, he began pawing around for the sock in the wet undergrowth, muttering aloud over his clumsiness.

"Who is there? Come out immediately."

Pieter froze. German-accented Dutch. Had to be the first patrol after curfew. How could he have been so stupid as to forget about that?

"Come out of there or I will shoot."

Pieter stood up, hands in the air. "I . . . I was looking for a book I dropped," he began, walking out on the road.

"Don't you know it's after curfew?" Pieter's heart jumped when he realized that he was facing the same two Moffen who'd taken Jan and Beppie's bicycles. There they were, now with tires on the wheels. No wonder he hadn't heard them ride up.

The shorter of the two soldiers stepped forward. "You look familiar," he said. "Have we spoken with you recently?"

"No," Pieter answered quickly. "Maybe you have seen my cousin. We look alike."

"And what is this cousin's name?"

"Oh, come on, Gottfried, who cares?" The other soldier steadied his bicycle. "Let's go have some supper."

Gottfried frowned at Pieter. "I'll let you go this time, but don't let me catch you out again. You know the rules. Go home and stay there."

"Yes, sir."

"And next time, I will remember your face." Then Gottfried got back on his bicycle, but didn't leave. "Go on," he said to Pieter. "Go home."

Pieter had no choice but to leave the sock full of bent smokes and hurry across the road. Worse yet, the Moffen were watching, waiting to see where he was going. He felt like a traitor for entering his own backyard and back door. Now the rotten Germans knew where he lived.

Inside, Pieter quickly locked the door, then sagged against it, breathing hard. Sweat poured down his arms and back, sweat that was hot with anger as well as fear. He caught his breath before he ran upstairs and found Mama by Jacob's bed. Jacob seemed to be asleep.

"Did you get much tobacco?" Mama whispered.

Pieter explained what had happened to it. "I'll go back as soon as it's safe," he said. "Right now I need to talk to someone about the soldiers on the train." His pulse began to race again.

"Tell me."

He saw Jacob staring at him, eyes wide with interest. Pieter bent over the bed.

"Tell me," Jacob whispered again.

"The train was long and full of soldiers. No lights. And I heard dogs." Now Pieter could see that Jacob's eyes were unnaturally bright, probably feverish.

"Which way . . . was it going?"

"South, in the direction of Overloon."

A pause, raspy breathing. Then, "Anything else? Anything at all?"

"Oh, yes. Maybe this is most important. Insignia, with '107' on shoulder patches and words beneath. I couldn't translate them."

The soldier's breath was louder. "'107,' you say?

58

That's the Ghost Brigade . . . crack armored troops."
He paused as if to gather strength. "Their tanks disappear into the trees after an attack. We . . . were
briefed . . . about them before . . . we jumped." He
forced out his words between deep breaths, and the
effort seemed to cost him. He closed his eyes and sank
further into the pillow.

The Ghost Brigade. Pieter had heard of them.
After a moment he had to ask. "What does it mean?
Is there going to be a battle south of here like the one
north at Arnhem?"

Jacob struggled with the bedcovers, as though he
wanted to get up but couldn't muster the strength. "I
don't know. But we Americans are moving up from the
south . . ." A pause for breath, then, "And our soldiers
need to know. What else . . . in the last few days?"
Jacob's face was flushed now; it glistened with sweat.

Mama began to wring out a washcloth in water.
Pieter watched her as he remembered. "Last Wednesday morning, we heard tanks traveling on the road.
Lots of them, going south."

"Word. We have to get word out fast." Jacob
pulled off the washcloth Mama had just put on his
forehead. "Your brother — where is he? Can we send
him a message?" He fell back onto the pillow.

If anyone knew how to reach Menno, it would be
Beppie, but Pieter didn't know where she was. He could
think of no one else to carry a message, except . . .

"I'll go," Pieter said to Jacob. "Give me the message, and I'll see that it's delivered."

To his own ears, his voice sounded amazingly

calm. But even as he spoke, he tasted something thick in his throat that had to be his own fear, clotting up inside him.

CHAPTER 10

A Second Message

Moments later

"Give me the exact message to carry," Pieter whispered again to Jacob.

"No!" Mama cried out. "You can't go. You're too young."

"I'm nearly as old as Beppie, and she is doing very dangerous things. She'd know what to do about this." Pieter's heart was not as bold as his words. But so many people depended on him now that he knew he had to bury his fear, hide it, fight it, not let it influence his decisions.

"Your mother said there is a traitor in this village," Jacob said faintly. "You are sure of this Beppie?"

Pieter felt as if he'd been slapped. Beppie? A traitor? He'd trust her with his life. It was the same trust he felt for his family and Jan, but no others. Not even Uncle Bro.

Jacob drifted away again, eyes closed, breath harsh and uneven. Mama bathed his face with the washcloth some more.

"This Beppie," Jacob began, eyes still closed. "She must be a schoolgirl."

Pieter looked at Mama and wondered how much he could say in front of her. He didn't want to frighten her any more than necessary. But Jacob should know everything.

"Beppie sent me to deliver a package to Auntie Riek."

"Auntie Riek." Jacob's eyes snapped open. "You know about her?"

"What sort of package?" Mama demanded.

Pieter didn't answer, too startled by Jacob's reaction. Auntie Riek must be the grandmother of someone important in the Resistance, someone who could be trusted. "Should I go to Auntie Riek again, tell her about the train?"

"No, you cannot go south now." Jacob struggled to sit up.

"Yes, listen to him," Mama pleaded. "You cannot go anywhere."

"Shortwave?" Jacob gasped. "Does this Beppie know of one?"

"Yes." Pieter would find one, with or without Beppie. "Tell me what to say."

"Paper, pencil, quickly." Jacob fell back on his pillow.

Pieter ran to his room and dug in his book bag for a scrap of paper and a pencil stub. When he came back, he saw that Mama was working on Jacob's bandage. There were fresh red spots on it.

"It's worse," Pieter said. "You need a doctor."

"No, no. The paper, quickly," Jacob said.

He wrote as Pieter and Mama watched. But the words were jumbled and made no sense.

"Shall I help with the spelling?" Pieter asked. "Our words are so tricky."

Jacob looked at him, eyes bright with fever. "It is code, Pieter."

Of course it was in code. Pieter felt so stupid. His face got hot, burned with embarrassment. Would he ever grow up?

"It's late," Mama said. "Surely this can wait until morning."

Jacob eased himself back on the pillow. "The war will not wait until morning, Mrs. van Dirk. I'm sorry to ask this of you and Pieter, but the message is urgent." Even speaking seemed to exhaust him, and he closed his eyes, hardly seeming to breathe.

Pieter put the message in his pocket and hurried downstairs. As he put on his jacket, Mama came in the kitchen. Without a word, she hugged him close. He could feel her trembling.

"I'll be back, Mama," he said. "I promise."

He stepped out into the night, more damp now that it was beginning to rain again. As he waited for his eyes to adjust to the darkness, he thought about what he would do. Go to Beppie's and see if she was home yet. If she wasn't, he would steal a bicycle and ride south to Auntie Riek's. He didn't know what else to do.

Pieter walked to the hawthorn hedge and peered through. The patrol wouldn't come this way for another hour, although that rotten Gottfried could be lurking somewhere, waiting to grab him. But the dark road stretched empty each way, and the tall grass leading to the railroad tracks waved rhythmically with the heavy touch of wet night air. Then he remembered the sock full of tobacco, and his heart leaped in alarm. He'd get that tomorrow, if it was still there.

Rain pummeled his back as he ran into the road, away from the shelter of house and trees and hedge. Turning toward the canal that bisected the village, he walked quickly across its bridge, then kept to the shadows as he followed the path to Beppie's house. Houses were scattered along this first block, but all were blanketed in dark silence now.

Suddenly Pieter heard squeaky bicycle rims bumping along the cobblestone street. He jumped into a deep doorway as the sound grew nearer. Was it the patrol already? No, they had tires for their bikes now, and this was a lone biker anyway. Germans were never alone on the streets after dark.

After the rider had passed by, Pieter stepped forward to look. The hulking back of a man dressed in a dark coat was just disappearing around the corner. Must be someone with a work permit or he'd never be out at this hour, unless he had friends in high Nazi places and nothing to fear.

Pieter walked on, and soon Beppie's house appeared just ahead. It was completely dark. He walked cautiously around to the back, remembering the upstairs from the other day when he'd changed his clothes in the spare bedroom. Yes, that was it, there. So which room was Beppie's, and which belonged to her parents?

He licked rain from his lips while he wondered what to do. In the dark he found some hard berries on a bush and pulled off a handful, wondering if he should throw them against the window that might be Beppie's.

But he couldn't make himself do it. He threw the berries on the ground, his insides slamming against his ribs, as if they were trying to escape his indecision. He knew he was stalling, hoping for some miracle that would tell him what to do. Oh, he'd sounded so brave and strong when he told Jacob he could handle this. But it was the biggest lie of the war. He only hoped that Jacob hadn't sensed his fear and hesitation.

But he had to work against his fear. He couldn't go home without doing something about the message in his pocket. No, he had to get a bicycle and go to Auntie Riek's by himself. Turning now toward the garden shed, he hoped against all odds that his bicycle was inside. Was it only last Wednesday that he'd left it here and ridden south to Auntie Riek's on Beppie's bicycle, dressed as a girl? It seemed so long ago.

The handle of the door squeaked as he turned it. But everything squeaked these days. It was part of the occupation, like rations and curfew. Now his anxiety grew in his throat, swelled up like a balloon. He would choke on it if the war didn't end soon.

He opened the door just far enough to squeeze

through the opening and found it even darker inside than out. Stretching out his arms, he felt for handlebars, wheels, anything that would tell him he'd found his bicycle.

Suddenly, out of the darkness, someone grabbed his arms, pinned them behind him, and kicked his legs out from under him. He slammed to the ground, dirt gritting in his mouth, pebbles scratching his cheeks as someone dug a knee into his back.

"Explain yourself," the voice said.

"Beppie?" Pieter gasped. "Oh, Beppie, where have you been?"

"Pieter?" The pressure on his back eased.

"Yes! Please let me up. I've been so worried. No one has seen you for days." He felt so relieved that she had returned, his body turned to mush. Now he wondered if he could stand, but he had to. He couldn't show weakness now, not in front of Beppie.

"You almost got yourself killed." Her voice was as sharp as glass splinters. "What are you doing here?"

He sat up, then quickly told her about Jacob and the message.

"American soldier?" Beppie asked. "You are sure of him?"

Pieter was stunned. "Of course I'm sure. Menno brought him to us." As he stood up and brushed himself off, he wondered why she couldn't trust him the way he trusted her. Then he couldn't resist. "The soldier wondered about you too, Beppie."

Beppie laughed softly, a small, tinkling sound that mixed with the drumming of rain on the shed's tin roof. "You are the only one I know who does not question, Pieter. I hope you survive the war with your trust still intact."

Now it was Pieter's turn to be insistent. "The message, Beppie. Jacob said it was urgent."

"Let's see it," Beppie said, then laughed softly again. "How can I see it in here?"

"He wrote it in code," Pieter offered. "Looked like my last spelling test."

Beppie seemed to be making up her mind before she asked, "You're sure you were not followed?"

Pieter wasn't sure of anything anymore. "Yes, I'm sure."

"Very well, then," she answered, picking up a basket made of wicker. "Let's go. I only hope you're not afraid of heights."

CHAPTER 11

A Fist against the Enemy

Moments later

Pieter slipped out of the garden shed behind Beppie, then picked his way across the yard, following her closely. Trees suddenly appeared like skinny ghosts against the dark night. Like ghosts, the night made no sound. It was too quiet, unreal, as if the silence held the night hostage. Even the light rain seemed to fall soundlessly now.

"Beppie, why were you hiding in the shed?" Pieter whispered after a while.

She paused to look at the yard next door. "I'd been to a meeting and wanted to watch my house before I went in. You know, make sure no one was waiting inside besides my parents."

He shuddered, every nerve alert, tingling. "This meeting," he began. "Is that where you've been since Wednesday?" She'd sidestepped the question before.

"Don't ask, Pieter. I can't answer. It is for your

safety. Don't you understand?" She sounded almost . . . nice.

"But what about my bike?" he asked. "What happened —"

"It was taken," she said tersely.

Oh, no, Pieter thought. The Moffen have taken my bike too. But he knew from the tone of Beppie's voice that he'd better not ask any more questions.

Beppie hurried down the path toward the canal now. Just before they crossed the bridge, she looked in every direction, then continued, with Pieter directly behind her. Would it always be this way? Pieter wondered. She led and he followed. She ordered and he obeyed.

"Come on, come on," Beppie's voice urged him.

Where were they going? Into town, it seemed. To Uncle Bro's tavern? People would be there at this hour; that would be normal. But they would probably be German soldiers, and no one, not even Beppie, would dare to send a message under their noses.

She led him in the other direction, stepping off the bridge and taking the cobblestone walk toward the church. The church, then. Of course. Pastor Kooiman must be the one who would send the message.

Inside they'd be safe, and the silence would be real, too. Only God could make noise in church at this hour. They would give the message to Pastor Kooiman and go home. Good.

Pieter patted his pocket with the message inside as he and Beppie stopped behind the shed in back. "Why are we waiting?"

"Quiet," Beppie whispered. She looked around once more, and so did Pieter. Rain-filled clouds hung on rooftops, the rain angling in such a direction that he could see little else. They needed Kazan now, he thought. Kazan with his big, wet nose that would sniff out anything for meters around. Oh, Kazan, where are you?

"Let's go," Beppie ordered.

The back door of the church opened easily, and they stepped into the hall behind the altar. Through an archway, Pieter saw a stub of candle glowing before the cross.

"Is it. . . . safe here?"

"Can you think of any place that is?" Beppie threw the words at him before she disappeared around the corner and up some steps.

Pieter followed, realizing with a jolt that they were climbing up to the steeple. He'd never been up there, but he'd heard about it from kids who'd done it on a dare. So this was what Beppie meant when she said she hoped he wasn't afraid of heights. Didn't she know he was afraid of everything?

There was no handrail as they went round and round up the steep stairs, and the walls closed in on Pieter until he thought the breath was being squeezed out of him. But Beppie didn't hesitate at all; she bounded up the steps above him.

"Come on." Her voice reached down. "We haven't got all night."

Pieter rounded the last step to see her figure dimly outlined in the open doorway to the steeple. When she saw him, she turned and stepped inside.

Pieter drew in a deep breath, then stepped into the enclosure. Immediately he saw the great church bells, silent since the occupation began.

No one else was there — just Beppie by the light of a candle stub opening a small metal box with some dials inside. Now she began to pull at some wires, and shortly an antenna appeared. It snapped together easily, and she adjusted it.

"How did you know it was here?" Pieter asked.

"It's my job to know." She looked at the slats closed tightly across the steeple openings. "I'll need the candle in order to send the message. But once I'm through, open some slats and watch for any movement below."

"You know how to use that transmitter?" Pieter pointed to the box. Two dials on it glowed in the darkness.

"Of course."

"But how . . ."

"First the message." Pieter handed it to her, and she scanned it briefly. Then, as Pieter watched in astonishment, Beppie began to tap out the signals on the key. When she finished, she blew out the candle. "Now, Pieter, open some slats and watch for anything that moves. Anything, understand?" She began to pack the transmitter into the wicker basket she had brought from home. "My mother used it for shopping," she said simply. "She doesn't need it now, since there is nothing to shop for."

"Don't we have to wait for a reply?"

"There won't be one."

71

"Then how do you know the message was received?"

"They are listening but cannot answer. It would give away their position. Now go and keep watch."

In the dark he worked his way around the bells to the steeple walls. Prying open some of the wooden slats, he looked down on the sleeping village and sensed the potential danger, but felt amazement too. He'd never been up this high in his life. Buildings appeared no larger than dollhouses, the canal a broad slash of ink across an old, dark painting. Rain stung his face as he watched for movement below.

"Do you send all the messages from here?" Pieter asked.

"No. Each time we send a message, we give away our position as well. The next message will be sent from another location."

To the right Pieter noticed how the road leading away from the village dipped into a gully, casting a narrow, deep shadow. Someone could hide there and watch, although he saw nothing now.

"Everything's ready," Beppie said. "Pieter, you go first. I'll follow."

"You want me to go first?" His nerves were on fire, and suddenly he shuddered violently. What if the Moffen had picked up their location already?

"It took you forever to get up here." Beppie's voice sounded like the thin edge of a steel knife. "Go, I say."

Pieter darted out of the doorway and hurtled down the steps. Around and around he ran, nearly out of control, barely touching the cold, hard steps until he was standing in the hall behind the altar. Flickery shadows danced across the wall as he sank against it. His breath ratcheted into his mouth from lungs that threatened to explode.

Suddenly Beppie was beside him, touched his shoulder briefly, then nodded toward the door. She walked to it, one hand holding the basket, the transmitter inside covered with a faded linen cloth, while the other closed on the doorknob and started to turn it.

"Wait!" Pieter cried out, barely a whisper. He grabbed her hand with a strength that surprised both of them. "Did you hear it?" He knew the sound of tire rim scraping on cobblestone as well as he knew the sound of his mother's voice. It was there, just beyond the door. Someone was riding past on the walkway behind the church.

"What is it?" she whispered back.

He told her about the man he'd seen earlier that night.

"Did you recognize him?"

"No."

"Do you think he followed you?"

"No, he couldn't have known I was there," Pieter answered. "I thought he was going home from work, but he must have a girlfriend at the other end of town instead."

"Well, maybe so." She didn't sound convinced. "But thanks, Pieter, for stopping me. Let's wait a few minutes more, to make sure he's gone."

They sank to the floor together and leaned against the door.

"How did you learn to send messages?" Pieter asked.

"My brother taught me," Beppie began, and her voice softened with remembrance. "When he was learning to be a telegrapher for the railroad, I watched and listened. After he discovered I had learned the international code that way, he let me practice on his key. Soon, my fist sounded just like his."

"Fist?"

"It's like a signature or a fingerprint. Every person who sends codes telegraphs in his own way or pattern. They call that a fist, and soon it is recognized. After my brother began to send messages for the Resistance, no one else from this village could do it because no one else sounded like him. Another fist couldn't be trusted. It might mean infiltration by the Moffen."

"Except for yours." Pieter understood.

"Except for mine," Beppie echoed. "After he was killed, I stepped in."

Pieter remembered two years ago when the Germans had taken hostages after the Resistance had bombed the railroad. Just taken railroad workers out and shot them in retaliation. Beppie's brother had been one of them.

"Now I send all the messages for the Resistance commander in this district," Beppie was saying. "And I won't stop until I send the most important one: That we are free."

"You should have told me, Beppie."

"No, and I shouldn't have told you even now. It's too dangerous for you to know so much."

Here was the real Beppie at last, not that hard, bossy girl who never listened. But she had listened tonight and even let him take the lead. And she had talked about herself and what made her take such chances with her life.

The warmth of his discovery stayed with Pieter all the way home. A few minutes after he stepped inside his own familiar kitchen, the mantel clock chimed twice. Two o'clock in the morning. He'd only been up this late once before in his life. It was the night the Germans had taken his father away.

Maybe tonight he'd helped do something to bring him home.

CHAPTER 12

A Matter of Trust

The next morning, September 25

Pieter had fallen into a heavy sleep that brought morning too soon. His mother's face slowly came into focus. She'd nearly come unraveled last night when he'd returned so late; this morning she seemed in charge of herself.

"You must wake up, Pieter," she said, her hand shaking his shoulder. "The American says this morning of all mornings you must go to school."

"Why?" Pieter struggled to rediscover that warm, soft spot on his pillow, holding on to the covers that Mama was tugging from him.

"The Germans will know that a message was sent," Mama said. "They will suspect anyone who is out of place, even a schoolboy tardy or absent from his classes."

Suddenly Pieter was wide awake. "I'm coming."

Mama gave his shoulder one final shake before she hurried from the room.

As Pieter dressed, he heard Jacob calling to him from across the hall.

"How did it go?" he asked when Pieter walked into the room. "The message . . . everything went okay?" The American's face looked sweaty and flushed.

"Yes." Pieter finished buttoning his shirt and sweater. "I watched and listened. Beppie is very good."

Jacob nodded wearily. "Maybe she will teach you one day."

Pieter wanted to say more, had questions to ask, but the soldier had closed his eyes, and his breathing seemed heavy. The questions would have to wait.

Pieter's stomach growled through morning classes, and his eyes burned from weariness. He tried to hide his yawns, propping his chin in his hands and staring as Mr. van der Meer droned on and on. He must have dozed off because suddenly he felt himself jerking violently awake. Then he saw his teacher staring at him.

During study period a little while later, Mr. van der Meer came to Pieter's desk. "Are you all right?" he asked. "You look very pale."

"I'm fine," Pieter answered. "Maybe I didn't have enough breakfast." That was true enough. Two small turnips that were hard and tasteless had been almost inedible.

"Yes, I understand." Mr. van der Meer patted his shoulder. "This war is so hard on my students, and I worry about each one of you." He smiled before he went back to his desk.

Pieter looked quickly out the window, longing to

be elsewhere. He felt so uncomfortable around that man. He was as slick as a greasy sausage.

When the noon bell rang, Pieter hurried outside. The damp chill made him fully alert now, and he looked around for Jan. He saw him coming across the schoolyard.

Jan's shoulders were hunched against the dampness as he walked up. "Pieter, you did nothing but yawn all morning. Do you know that Mr. Potato Eyes was watching you every minute?"

"Yes. He said the war was hard on me, and even you." Pieter gave Jan a playful poke.

A knowing look crossed Jan's face as he thumped Pieter on the back. "Hey, now I know why you're so sleepy. You were with Beppie last night, weren't you? And we know what you'd like to do with her, don't we?"

Pieter felt his face flame. Jan knew how he felt about Beppie, but was Jan talking about that or about her Resistance work?

"Come on, Jan," Pieter said, lamely. "If anybody finds out, I'll never hear the end of it."

"Your secret is safe with me. Don't you know that?" Jan's manner had changed now. He was serious, not teasing or kidding around. He knows, Pieter thought. He really knows.

"Did you hear the Germans are moving more troops south of here?" Jan whispered. "Ma heard it when she stood in line for milk this morning. She even woke up Pa to tell him, but he had such a hangover from that rotten beer your Uncle Bro sells, he didn't care what the Moffen did for once."

How did the news get around so fast? Pieter wondered. Aloud, he said, "What's so important down south?"

"British troops are headed in the same direction," Jan said, blowing on his hands. "At least that's what the big rumor is."

Back in class after lunch, Pieter wondered about the news Jan had shared. If the news about the troop train could be on the street so quickly this morning, it was very likely known last night. So there would be no reason to be in such a hurry to send a message about only that. No, Jacob's message had more in it than just the train's movements and the identity of the troops on it. But what was it? Maybe Jacob would be alert enough this afternoon to tell him.

After school, as Pieter slipped through the hedge into his own backyard, he glanced up toward Menno's room and saw his mother's face in the window. The moment she saw him she disappeared, and Pieter knew she must be hurrying to the back door. What had happened?

He met Mama in the doorway. She pulled him quickly inside, then closed and locked the door.

"Nobody's found out about Jacob, have they?" Pieter's breath choked in his throat.

"No." Mama fought for control of her voice. "Oh, Pieter, the American is so much worse. His fever is higher than ever, and he doesn't speak, just tosses back and forth. I'm so worried."

Pieter ran upstairs to the bedroom and saw Jacob

covered with sweat, his face pasty. The bedcovers were thrown back in tangled heaps, the sheets torn from the mattress by his thrashing. Now he began to moan and call out.

When Pieter removed the bandage on Jacob's shoulder, he gagged at the stench. Pus oozed from the bullet wound, while the skin around it was bright red.

He glanced at the basin of water and the cloth on the bedside table. Mama had been trying, but it wasn't enough. Nothing would be enough now but a doctor and some real medicine.

"I don't know what else to do," Mama said, as she hurried into the room.

"I'll get Dr. Prager." Pieter turned to go.

"No!" Mama's voice was low but emphatic. "The Germans supply him with brandy in exchange for their soldiers' medical care. We can't trust him."

"I'll tell him that you're sick."

"But when he comes, he'll know. He might report us to the Nazis."

"It's a chance we have to take." Pieter sighed wearily.

"I'm so tired of worrying about the Germans," Mama whispered. "When will it ever end?" She fell back into a chair and covered her face with her hands.

"Stop it, Mama." Pieter's voice was harsh, but there was no time for tears now. "Take care of Jacob until I come back. Look, you're disturbing him."

Pieter's words made Mama look up. "Of course, I should be thinking of him, not myself. And you,

Pieter. I should be thinking of you. You are still a schoolboy."

The front doorbell rang. "Are you expecting someone, Mama?"

"No." Her eyes grew wide and fearful. "No one." She stood up, stood close to him.

Pieter's heart pounded like dull thunder. Maybe it was Beppie bringing news about last night. But if it wasn't . . .

Downstairs he opened the door, trying to keep a smile on his face as he stared up into Mr. van der Meer's eyes. "Oh, sir, I was just leaving."

"Surely you have one moment for your teacher." Without waiting, Mr. van der Meer stepped inside. "Is your mother here?"

"She is resting." Pieter licked his dry lips and felt sweat gather under his arms. What if Jacob moaned or cried out again?

"And you, Pieter, shouldn't you be resting, too? You seem so tired, and it's affecting your schoolwork. Your mother should know."

What's going on here? Pieter wondered. Why is he making such a fuss over my schoolwork? Only one grade was lower than the rest, and that was a month ago.

They heard the noise at the same time. "What was that?" Mr. van der Meer looked toward the stairs.

"I think my mother wants something. If you'll excuse me . . ."

Mr. van der Meer turned to the door. "You must go to her, then. But I would like a word with her as

81

soon as she can see me." He held out his hand, and Pieter was forced to take it. "Good-bye," he said before he opened the door.

Mr. van der Meer had parked his bicycle by the front door. Now he hopped on it and pedaled down the street without a backward glance. Pieter watched, listening to the bike's rims squeak on the cobblestones. Another sound of war, he thought.

CHAPTER 13

Too Much to Ask

Moments later

Pieter left the house as soon as he dared, pausing at each corner to be sure Mr. van der Meer was nowhere in sight. He only hoped his teacher hadn't stayed around to spy. What would Mr. Potato Eyes do if he learned an American paratrooper was lying wounded in Menno's bed and in need of a doctor? But never mind Mr. van der Meer now. The important thing was to try to save Jacob.

Pieter tried to look casual as he walked along the canal, tried not to hurry. But his insides were churning, and he was sure his face gave him away. He was glad for the near darkness, glad the days had grown shorter and the sky matched the color of his dark blue coat, patches and all.

Would Dr. Prager have anything left in his medicine bag to treat an infection like Jacob's? Just remembering the look and smell of the wound made Pieter's stomach lurch. He knew Dr. Prager had helped villagers from time to time since the occupation, but as medical supplies had dwindled, so had his practice. Maybe the old doctor knew of something they had done in the long-ago days with roots or leaves. The American just couldn't die.

Two canal crossings later, Pieter saw Dr. Prager's house at the next corner. It seemed to have shrunk. The bricks sagged closer to the foundation, and the roof tiles looked caved in; a few were broken. Only a dim light in the kitchen showed that someone still lived there.

Pieter knocked on Dr. Prager's weathered, peeling door. Why didn't he come? The old man had to be there. No one wasted candles on an empty room.

Pieter pounded again before a key turned in the lock.

"Dr. Prager?" Pieter didn't recognize him. His face had withered into creases, and behind his wire-rimmed glasses, the doctor's eyes were watery and out of focus.

"Yes, yes, what do you want?" His voice sounded reedy, and his words were slurred.

So it was true. The rumors about his drinking were true.

"I'm Pieter van Dirk." He felt sweaty inside his shirt. He was wasting time with this delay. "You and my father . . ." They had been elders in church together, friends, but what did that matter now?

Dr. Prager opened the door wider. "Of course," he shouted suddenly. "They took your father away. Then they killed my wife."

Pieter grabbed Dr. Prager before he fell, then pushed him inside and closed the door. "You mustn't talk this way," he began.

"Do you know what today is?" Dr. Prager's breath could start a fire. "Today it is two years since my wife died because of them. Come, come with me."

He dragged Pieter into the kitchen, his grip strong and unrelenting. A candle stub glowed on the table before an oval picture of a blonde woman Pieter vaguely remembered. Globs of wax dotted the table, suggesting the doctor had spent many nights here.

"Two years ago," Dr. Prager went on, "the Moffen would not give us travel passes so that I could take Trinka to the hospital in Overloon. Without the surgery, she died. They did it. They killed her."

Pieter noticed the bottle of German brandy on the table, half-empty. Maybe it wasn't too late. Maybe Mama would know how to sober him up. Why did people try to blot out their feelings with drinking? Jan's father did it, too. Maybe it was the only way for some people to get through the war.

But Pieter knew he couldn't wait any longer. "My mother is sick, Dr. Prager. You've got to help her."

"No. I have no medicine, not even in my head."

"Please. I know you can help. There is no one else."

Dr. Prager blinked rapidly several times. "No, I am of no use to anyone. Even after the war, there will be nothing left for me. Nothing to work for, to hope for. Don't you understand?"

"No!" Pieter shouted, feeling out of control. "I

don't understand. Your own people need you, Dr. Prager. But you just take care of the Germans for liquor. You're nothing but a drunk old coward."

Pieter stalked out of the house, slammed the door, then turned and kicked it hard. He'd never talked like that before to anyone, and now, he didn't care that he had. He kicked the door again, knowing he was making a disturbance. Let someone call the Germans. Bring them all — he'd fight them one by one. How could Dr. Prager give up while everyone around him was struggling so hard to live?

Pieter charged down the street, his feelings boiling over like Mama's copper kettle. He couldn't face her and Jacob, tell them that no help was coming. Where else could he go? Who else could he ask to help? Aunt Gerda? Uncle Bro?

Pieter began to run toward the tavern, noticing only now how dark it had become as he stumbled over some cobblestones. But he suddenly stopped half a block away. Even from this distance he could see two German trucks parked outside, and he didn't dare go in and risk a wrong look or word. Reluctantly he turned toward home.

Then he thought of Beppie. Of course, she would know of a doctor who could be trusted. But first he would stop and reassure Mama.

At home he let himself in the back door with his key and ran upstairs to Menno's bedroom. "Beppie?" She was the last person he expected to see here. "How . . . I mean, why?" Then he looked at Jacob, whose face glistened with sweat. "He's worse, isn't he? Where's Mama?"

86

Beppie stood up and motioned for Pieter to follow her into the hall. "When I came to see you, your mother told me you had gone for Dr. Prager. I offered to sit with Jacob while she rested. Is the doctor coming?"

"No." Pieter slumped against the wall as he told her. "Do you know of anyone we can get, Beppie? Maybe you can call someone on the shortwave."

She shook her head. "It's about the transmitter that I'm here," she said. "I was going to move it to its new hiding place tonight, but I had to change my plans."

"Why?"

"The new location is being watched, Pieter."

"Where is the transmitter now?"

Beppie looked at him without answering. Then he understood.

"I know. I ask too many questions. You've told me often enough. But why did you come here?"

"To ask if you would keep the transmitter for a while."

Pieter straightened up so quickly that he banged his head against the wall. "Me? You want me to keep the . . . the . . ." He couldn't get the word out. How could he do that? Where could he hide it? "I can't, Beppie. It's too much to ask."

"Pieter." Beppie spoke softly, her hand touching his arm. "My usefulness may be at an end. Too many people have noticed when I come and go. But you, Pieter — you are still above suspicion. You have only been a courier once, and you were dressed as a girl. . . . So you're safe for now."

For now, she said. How long would that last? But how could he refuse? Beppie needed his help — now.

A sound from Jacob brought Pieter back to the moment. "We'll have to talk about this later," he whispered. "I've got to get some help for the American."

"There is a doctor near Boxmeer we can trust, but it may take a while to reach him," Beppie said. "I can't use the transmitter now, I know that."

"Then I'll get a bike and go for him." He would steal one if he had to. From Mr. van der Meer, or maybe Jan would let him take his father's. Pieter made a move toward the stairs. "Give me his address." Brave talk. But he had no choice anymore. And he had a feeling he was doing this for more than Jacob. He was doing it for Menno and Gerrit and Papa, and yes, even for Kazan.

They hurried into the kitchen. "Do I need directions? Is this doctor in Boxmeer, or the country or . . ."

A tapping sound came at the back door, so faint that Pieter wondered if he'd imagined it. Until he looked at Beppie, and then his heart froze. She'd heard it too.

"Kazan used to do that." It felt safe to think of him. "He . . . he always tapped with his paw."

"Forget the dog," Beppie whispered. "It's the Moffen. I must have been followed."

"They wouldn't tap." Pieter knew that from the night Papa had been taken away. "They'd just come in."

The tapping began again, harder this time.

Beppie's words were stone-hard. "See who it is. I'll be right behind you."

Pieter put his hand on the doorknob, drew in a deep, trembling breath, and pulled the door open.

CHAPTER 14

A Traitor among Us

A moment later

"Dr. Prager!" Pieter nearly shouted.

"Shhh," Beppie ordered and pulled the doctor inside. Just as quickly she shut the door and locked it.

"He smells of liquor," she said. "Was it wise to ask him here?"

Dr. Prager sat down at the kitchen table and rested his head in his hands. A stethoscope dangled from his jacket pocket. "Give me a moment and I will be all right," he said.

"Get your mother," Beppie whispered to Pieter.

He ran upstairs and found Mama back at Jacob's bedside. "Downstairs, Mama. Quickly," he whispered. "We have a problem." He ran downstairs again, with Mama following.

Beppie had Dr. Prager on his feet and was walking him back and forth across the kitchen. "I've heard this helps," she said. "But he seems so drunk."

Mama moved across the room in three quick steps. "How dare you!" she said to the doctor. Then she slapped his face, hard. "How dare you allow yourself this indulgence when you are needed so much?"

Slowly Dr. Prager's eyes focused on Mama. "I thought you were ill," he said. "Did I misunderstand?"

"First, it is coffee for you." Mama walked to the stove and began to coax a small flame from the embers. "But even if I had real coffee, I would not give it to you. You deserve what the Germans have left us, nothing more." Then she slammed a cup on the table as if it were a weapon.

Pieter was transfixed. He'd seldom seen Mama this way.

"Did you bring any medicine?" Beppie asked.

Dr. Prager shook his head. "She doesn't seem to need anything."

"You know I am not your patient." Now Mama viciously pounded acorns on a marble slab.

"Then who?" Dr. Prager seemed to be waking from some long dream, perhaps a nightmare.

"Can we trust you?" Beppie demanded.

"After what the Germans did to my Trinka, you can still ask that?"

"Drunks have little control of their tongues." Beppie walked around to stand in front of him.

"I haven't always been like this," he answered. "Tell the young ones, Lida."

Mama turned from the stove. "Yes, that's right." Mama paused, as if she were making up her mind about him. Then she nodded. "He will be all right after

91

I am through with him. Pieter, go up to Jacob. Beppie, help me with the doctor."

Pieter ran upstairs, glad to be out of the way. He could only imagine what Mama was going to do to sober up Dr. Prager.

He hurried to Jacob's bedside, rinsed out a cloth in cool water, and put it on the American's forehead. But what good was this? He needed more, maybe even more than a sober Dr. Prager.

Jacob mumbled something, a mixture of Dutch and, Pieter guessed, English, too.

Pieter leaned over him. "What did you say?" Then he noticed the red streak running down the soldier's arm. It looked as if someone had drawn a line in red ink on it. That was new.

Suddenly Jacob woke up. He grabbed Pieter's arm with amazing strength. "The message! Did it get through? Has anyone answered?"

Pieter pulled free, ashamed that the stench from Jacob's wound nauseated him. "Not yet, but someone will soon."

Jacob relaxed his grip on Pieter's arm. "It's so hot for September. It was always cold for Yom Kippur."

"We need fresh air," Pieter said and rushed to open the window so he could breathe in the cold, bracing air.

"That feels good," Jacob murmured. "I am so hot, but now I'm better."

His bandage had loosened, and, as Pieter tried to replace it, Jacob suddenly wrenched free. The bandage fell away and Pieter nearly vomited at the sight of the wound. It oozed pus, and the flesh around it was swollen and bloody.

Pieter forced himself to place a towel over Jacob's arm. "Tell me about life in America," he whispered. Maybe talking would calm him down until the doctor came, if he came.

"Baseball," Jacob whispered after a moment. "Firecrackers . . . Fourth of July." His voice faded.

"When did you go there?" Pieter asked. He had to keep him talking.

"Twelve. Hitler coming for all Jews, Pa said. Even Holland, unless . . ."

"Unless what?" Pieter leaned closer. "Someone stopped him?"

"Yes," Jacob whispered. "So I came back. To stop him."

"How did you meet my brother?" Pieter waited for an answer, but none came. "Jacob?" He didn't answer. "Jacob, listen. I'll talk now." Pieter touched his hand, then shook it. "Listen. I'll tell you about my dog. Oh, please, don't . . . I mean, stay here, don't die . . . don't . . ." Pieter was near panic now. Jacob was slipping away, and he couldn't stop him. He turned hopefully when he heard footsteps on the stairs. Mama came first, then Beppie, and then, thank God, the doctor. He looked terrible, but he also looked sober.

"Do something!" Pieter cried out.

Dr. Prager saw the red streak on Jacob's arm. "Blood poisoning," he said. "Boil water and get fresh cloths." He began to pull supplies from his jacket pockets. He put his stethoscope around his neck, laid out a pack of sharp, knife-like instruments on the bedside table, and set small vials of powders in a row. Then he pulled a bottle of brandy from his pocket.

"No!" Pieter shouted. "No!"

"This is for my patient, not me," Dr. Prager explained. "It is the only disinfectant I have left. What I am going to do now will not be pleasant to watch," he went on. "If you young ones want to leave, that is all right. Lida, I will need you." Then he turned to Jacob without another word. If he noticed the Star of David around Jacob's neck, he gave no sign.

Downstairs, Pieter put water in the kettle to boil for Dr. Prager, glad for something to do. Beppie sat down at the kitchen table and picked up the empty jam jar, turning it around in her hands. Was she as hungry as he was?

"Beppie, do you think it's possible that Dr. Prager could be the traitor?" Pieter asked. He sat down opposite her. "In spite of what happened to his wife?"

Beppie shrugged. "Anything is possible."

"Then you don't know who the traitor in the village is?" He was asking more questions again, but he couldn't help it.

"I'm not sure. Not exactly. Not yet." Then Beppie smiled. "And of course I wouldn't tell you. But I've decided to put the transmitter somewhere else before I go, Pieter. I won't leave it here after all."

"Go? Where are you going?" He wanted to know that more than what she planned to do with the transmitter.

"I'm not sure."

"Let me go with you."

"No, you're needed here. You've got to stay."

After the water came to a rolling boil, Pieter carried it up to the doctor. When he returned, Pieter found Beppie resting her head on her arm on the table, sleeping. He walked over and touched her hair. It was soft and silky, and curled easily around his fingers. He wanted to stand there forever, holding those strands of her hair so she would never leave.

Near dawn, Dr. Prager came downstairs, looking exhausted. At the sound of his footsteps, Beppie woke up, immediately alert. "Are you all right?" she asked him.

"I've never been so tired." He leaned against a chair. "But at the same time, I haven't felt quite so wonderful in years. I think I may have saved the young man's life upstairs." He allowed himself a smile, then spoke briskly. "Now I have to go home before the sun rises. The Germans might be suspicious if they see me walking upright in the morning when, for the last two years, I have been too drunk to stand."

Beppie got up, shaking her curls in place. "I'll walk with you, doctor. You look as if you could use a shoulder to lean on. Wait just a minute while I get my basket."

Pieter watched as Beppie went to the pantry and brought out her mother's shopping basket. Suddenly he knew what she was going to do. In his exhausted state, Dr. Prager would welcome Beppie's helping him into his house. Once she was inside, she would find a place where the transmitter would be well hidden.

The Germans wouldn't suspect the doctor who treated them, and Dr. Prager wouldn't report the transmitter even if he found it. Not unless he got drunk again. But it was a risk they all had to take, and they ought to be used to it by now. Dutchmen had been taking risks like this since the occupation began.

Checkmate, Beppie. Checkmate.

CHAPTER 15

Everyone a Suspect

Tuesday, September 26

It seemed to Pieter that he had barely fallen asleep when his mother shook him awake. This time she didn't have to tell him how important it was for him to show up at school. Before he left, Pieter stepped into Menno's room to say good morning to Jacob, but he was sleeping. His face still looked slightly feverish, but he was quieter now. No more restless thrashing around and crazy talk that didn't connect. Whatever Dr. Prager had done must have worked, but the American soldier wasn't going anywhere for a while, that was for sure. Not after what he'd been through.

Pieter would miss him after he left, but Jacob's presence in the house continued to be a real threat to his mother's safety as well as his own. If Dr. Prager got drunk again, he might say anything. And Mr. van der Meer was just too nosy. Did he know about Jacob, or just suspect something? Did anyone else know? Of course, Pastor Kooiman. He was the one who had told Mama about Menno. He had to know about the soldier, too.

As Pieter walked to school, he felt the sun warm his back, and some of his tension slowly melted away. But he knew the feeling wouldn't last. It was as temporary as the sun. Clouds hovered nearby, and before long the sun would disappear for weeks at a time, draining everything of warmth and color.

Pieter left the canal path and turned in the direction of the schoolyard, two blocks away. The church came into full view from this corner, and there, near the shed in back, stood Koos, looking up at the steeple.

Pieter's tension returned, sending a steel shaft up his spine. Had someone been talking about the shortwave transmission from the steeple? Koos must have heard rumors down at the tavern and decided to check it out for himself.

Pieter felt a soft tap on his shoulder and a whispered "Hey." He whirled around to find Jan looking at him with an expression Pieter didn't recognize. What was going on with Jan lately? He'd been acting different.

"What's the idea of scaring me like that?" Pieter whispered back. "Stop sneaking up on me."

"Looks like you're the one being sneaky, spying on your own cousin."

"Maybe you're right." If Pieter began to suspect his best friend now, he'd know he was ready for the crazy castle.

"What are you really doing, Pieter?"

"Watching Koos, that's all."

"Let's see if I got this right. You're watching Koos, who's watching the church steeple."

"I know it sounds strange." How could Pieter explain anything without giving away the transmitter, and how Beppie had taken it away, and that someone might have found out about the message sent Sunday night, and . . . oh, no. Could someone be up there now, just watching and waiting for the Resistance to do something careless?

"Does Koos think the steeple is going to move anytime soon?" Jan asked. "To Rotterdam, maybe? I hear they need new steeples there. In fact, they need a new city since the Germans bombed the old one to pieces."

Despite himself, Pieter began to laugh at Jan's dark sense of humor. It started as a snicker but quickly turned into a full-blown belly-stretcher. Then Jan started, and they fell over each other, laughing and pounding each other on the back. When Pieter stopped for a moment to wipe his eyes with his jacket sleeve, he saw Koos staring at them.

"Koos, wait," Pieter called.

But Koos didn't wait. After one more glance at the silvery rooftop of the steeple pointing silently to the sky, Koos turned quickly in the direction of school and hurried away. Who knew what went on in that head of his? He might know something important, or nothing at all.

"I guess Koos didn't think we were funny," Jan said, wiping his face with his sweater sleeve.

"Maybe we weren't." Pieter felt temporarily drained, emptied of anything he'd ever felt during the war. But he knew the fear and the anger would come surging back, just as they always did.

Pieter tried to keep his mind on his lessons during class, but his thoughts kept slipping back to Koos. If he knew something, that meant others did, too. People in the Resistance wouldn't talk openly, but someone else might. And they might not have known that Koos was listening.

When Pieter glanced up from his math book, he saw Mr. van der Meer staring at him. Not again. Suddenly Pieter had an overwhelming desire to stick out his tongue and make a monster face at the teacher. But, after a moment of temptation to misbehave, Pieter yawned instead, deliberately and noisily, before he went back to his book.

Let Mr. Potato Eyes make something of that.

The day plodded on, each moment as wearying as the last. Pieter felt tired and hungry all the time now. There wasn't enough food, partly because he hadn't gone back for the sock of bent smokes — he hadn't dared. He wasn't getting enough sleep, either. And lately, when he did sleep, he'd begun to dream about food: noodles and pot roast followed by one of Mama's berry cakes with plenty of thick cream on top. When he was in the middle of one of these dreams, he always woke up, and then he was hungrier than ever.

Did Jacob dream about food? he wondered. Or Menno or Gerrit or Papa? Were they more hungry than he was? He decided that when everyone came home from the war, the first meal they would have would begin at breakfast and not end until bedtime. Let it come soon, he thought. Let it come soon.

A special prayer service was called for the next afternoon. Was it really that or something else? Did Pastor Kooiman know something? Or was it a trick to get everyone there and then — Pieter didn't want to finish the thought, but his mind raced with possibilities. Maybe the Germans had set it up. Or maybe it was the work of the traitor himself.

The sun struggled to shine again as Pieter and Mama walked to church.

"Do you know what this is all about?" Mama asked.

"No." Pieter unbuttoned his jacket. "But we just have to act as if everything is normal. If we stayed home, I'd have to think up some lie to tell people, and I'm no good at lying."

"I'm relieved to hear you say that, Pieter," Mama smiled.

Inside the church, sunshine fingered its way through cracks in the stained-glass windows. Pieter looked longest at the shimmering ray spotlighting Beppie's golden hair before he sighed. She was still here, then. Maybe she'd decided not to go away until she knew more about this meeting.

Pastor Kooiman had begun a prayer that seemed to have no end. He droned on and on. Was it Pieter's imagination that the preacher was taking more time to get to the point? Despite his concern, Pieter's eyes closed, and slowly he began to drift away. He was outdoors in the sunshine, real sunshine that warmed him deep inside. He was playing with Kazan in a meadow where tulips grew everywhere. It was so beautiful.

Somewhere a door opened, but Pieter couldn't see a door in the meadow. Not in his dream, anyway. And it was so quiet. Why wasn't Pastor Kooiman talking anymore? That had been all right. He had allowed Pastor Kooiman to rumble on in his dream as a kind of background to everything else.

Pieter opened his eyes halfway and focused on Pastor Kooiman. He was stone-still, his eyes riveted to the back of the church. Was he having a vision, like one of the saints Pieter had read about?

Mama gave Pieter a sharp jab with her elbow. "Pieter, wake up. For heaven's sake, wake up."

Pieter didn't need to be told. He wakened completely now as boots, heavy boots, marched on the stone floor down the aisle. He knew, without glancing around, who it was. Now they came into his line of sight. Two German soldiers marched toward the pulpit, their boots making the only sound. The entire congregation seemed to have stopped moving, not breathing as they watched and waited.

The soldiers stopped in front of Pastor Kooiman. "You are under arrest," one of them said. "Come with us."

Pastor Kooiman had turned gray. He seemed to match the color of the church walls. "I have done nothing," he whispered. But his words carried to every corner.

"You secreted an illegal transmitter on the premises," the soldier droned on.

"I have no transmitter," Pastor Kooiman said. "There is no . . ."

"Come along." The soldiers stepped up beside the pastor, took him by the arms, and led him down the steps and then up the aisle. As they passed each row of pews, people turned to watch in complete silence. When the soldiers and Pastor Kooiman had disappeared out the church doors, people continued to sit, silent, stunned by what they'd just witnessed.

A warning, Pieter realized. This was a warning that the Moffen still controlled them. Finally Pieter had to move. He stood up, and then, as if on cue, everyone else did too. People began to talk and whisper around him. They huddled closely in the aisles, grouping together to feel safe.

"Excuse me," he said, again and again, trying to move past the knots of people crowding the aisles. He had to find Beppie, ask her about what had happened, find out what she'd want to do next. But when he reached the pew where she'd been sitting, he found only her parents.

Of course — she'd gone to the shed. She knew they couldn't talk openly. Even the trees had ears now, just as the steeple must have had eyes.

He hurried up the aisle, trying to appear as normal as anyone would at a time like this. Outside, parishioners talked on even as they watched the soldiers drive away with Pastor Kooiman. Jan and his father talked with Mr. van der Meer; Uncle Bro and Aunt Gerda were huddled with Mama and Dr. Prager.

Quickly Pieter slipped around to the back of the church, and a moment later he was inside the shed. "Beppie," he whispered. "Beppie." But he already knew she wasn't there. She was gone, really gone this time.

CHAPTER 16

Hare and Hounds

Thursday, September 28

The next day, Pieter's classmates spoke of little else than Pastor Kooiman's arrest. Had he been sent to Westerbork, too? Pieter wondered. So many people had been forced to go to that labor camp. So many, in fact, that it might have a bigger Dutch population than Amsterdam by now.

Pieter kicked at a stone on the path as he started home. Where had Beppie gone? If only he could ask someone about her. He doubted she'd told her parents where she was going. It was too dangerous for them to know. And there was no one else that he could trust to ask about her.

As he reached the village square, Pieter became aware of Koos following him. But he made no move to catch up, just followed as Pieter walked past empty shops and cafes catering to German soldiers.

Koos was such a puzzle. When they were younger,

it was easier for Pieter to accept him as he was — slow, simple, easy to handle. But now, since Koos had grown and gotten bigger, Pieter expected him to act older. He had to remind himself that Koos never would act much different, that he'd always see life as a kid with a kid's understanding.

After several more minutes, Pieter decided to confront Koos, find out if he wanted to talk about what happened in church yesterday. Koos might even know something that Pieter could piece together, if only from his cousin's mixed-up understanding of it.

He waited for Koos to approach. "We're too big to play follow-the-leader the way we did when we were first-graders," Pieter began. "Tell me what it is you're doing."

"You're not the only one with secrets," Koos said, stuffing his hands deep into the pockets of his brown pants. "I've got secrets, too."

"Who said I had any secrets?" Pieter asked. "I don't."

"Yes, you do. I've seen you doing stuff you shouldn't, and then you told me it was a secret."

Pieter's mind raced frantically. Koos knew about the bent smokes, but did he know something else? Koos hadn't seen him up in the steeple with Beppie, had he? Maybe he was the one riding by that night. Or Jacob. Was there some way he knew about the soldier?

"I'm not as dumb as you think, Pieter." Koos sounded really angry now. "I know a lot of stuff." He turned and began to walk across the canal bridge.

"Wait," Pieter called out. But Koos was running now, running for the only safety he knew, the tavern and his ma and pa.

Pieter ran to catch up with him. Koos could blurt out anything once he got inside, and anyone could be there. It was a public place, after all.

"Pieter, wait for me." He heard Jan's voice calling to him across the square.

"Can't stop," Pieter called back. "Have to go to Uncle Bro's. Family stuff."

"Me, too." Jan ran up and began to hurry alongside him. "I've got family stuff to do at the tavern, too. Ma wants Pa to come home right away before he drinks any more of that rotten beer your uncle serves."

Koos slammed the tavern door ahead before Pieter could reach him.

"What's wrong with Koos?" Jan asked.

"Who can tell?" Pieter said, his hand on the doorknob, bracing himself. Quickly he opened the door and stepped into the dark, smoky room, searching for his cousin. Where was he?

Jan hurried past Pieter. "Pa," he said. "Ma says you are to come home now."

Pieter looked toward the bar. Mr. de Waard sat there next to Mr. van der Meer. Dr. Prager sat alone, but he had no glass in his hand, and no bottle on the bar in front of him.

"Tell your mama I'll be along presently." Mr. de Waard's voice rolled easily toward them. "I want to get all the news."

"What news?" Pieter asked.

Uncle Bro spoke from the other end of the bar. "Beppie's father has been taken to Nazi headquarters in Venray for questioning about the transmitter."

"Why Beppie's father?" Pieter felt as if he'd been struck.

Uncle Bro cleared his throat. "Well, perhaps they think it's a family occupation. His son, you remember, operated the shortwave for the railroad."

They all know about Beppie, Pieter thought. Someone might as well have said it aloud. But do they know that I was with her in the church steeple when she sent her last message?

"Is Beppie that pretty girl who goes to our church?"

Pieter glanced over at Mr. van der Meer. "Yes, sir."

"She must go to *Huishoud* School, for girls only," Mr. van der Meer went on. "I've not seen her at our school."

"She's Pieter's girlfriend," Koos said. Where had he been standing all this time?

"And that's not all." Koos stepped nearer to the bar, nearer to Uncle Bro. "I know what they do at church."

"I . . . I guess your little romance isn't a secret anymore, Pieter." Uncle Bro quickly began to rearrange some glasses on the counter.

Mr. de Waard laughed. "Pieter, it must be hard to have a romance with a girl who disappears from time to time. Are you sure she doesn't have another boyfriend somewhere else?"

"Maybe she's taking a holiday." Jan glanced uneasily at Pieter.

"A holiday from the war?" Mr. van der Meer asked, with a touch of sarcasm. "How nice."

"She needs to be told about her father," Dr. Prager said.

"Pieter can tell her. I bet he knows where she is." Koos became bolder now, stepping into the center of the room.

"Don't bet on it, Koos," Pieter answered. "You'd lose."

A heavy silence descended on the room, heavier than the smoke from last night's fire. Pieter looked around to see everyone staring at him, watching, waiting. All those faces, all familiar, all known, some loved, but suddenly strangers all. He couldn't trust one of them now. Something had been said, words spoken that set off warning sounds in his head. He was almost certain that the traitor from the village was in this room.

Pieter felt suddenly light-headed. At first he thought it was because he was so hungry, although his body ought to be used to that by now. Then he realized that his weakness came from a feeling of danger he hadn't felt before. Worse, he couldn't look at anyone, not even Jan, for reassurance, because he might be looking directly into the eyes of the enemy, or someone who knew the enemy's identity.

"I have lots of homework," Pieter began. "I need to get started." His words, even his voice sounded hollow, but it was the best he could do. He opened the door and waited. Was no one going to say anything?

"Bye, Pieter," Koos called out. "See you tomorrow."

"Yes, tomorrow," Pieter said, closing the door. "If there is a tomorrow," he whispered, as he walked away.

Pieter hovered near Jacob during the evening, hoping there'd be a few moments when he could talk to him alone. He'd know what to do about a traitor. But during the short periods Jacob was awake, Mama would fuss over his covers or bandage, or give him something warm to drink. Then he would fall into a deep sleep again.

Finally Pieter went to his room and tried to study. But he couldn't concentrate, couldn't even see the words on the page. All he could see was Beppie's face. How he needed her here to tell him what to do!

He stood up, walked to the window, and looked out into the backyard. Although it was nearly dark, he saw the familiar shadows easily, shadows he'd looked at every night of his life before he went to bed. The one lone elm spiked the sky; the hedge at the back clumped together like tired old men on a park bench. Always the same, the same for thirteen years now. Well, not exactly. In the last few years they had cut down two of the trees for firewood, and soon the last elm would be gone too. What else was different now?

Pieter suddenly focused on a corner of the yard nearest the road. Had something moved? Yes, a dark shadow that had never been there before had just faded into the elderberry bush. Pieter jumped back, out of sight.

Someone was watching and waiting out there. A friend would come to the door and knock. An enemy wouldn't. An enemy watched and waited for something to happen. Only the traitor would wait for Pieter to make the next move.

Pieter went over to his desk and sat down, but studying was a thing of the past. Now he had to think of a plan. If only Beppie were here . . . but she wasn't. Get over it, he told himself. She isn't here, and it's all up to you now. A drumming began in Pieter's head, slow and insistent, as he tried to override his fear and come to a decision.

He was almost certain he knew who the traitor was, who was out there. It almost made it easier because he knew what the traitor knew and could plan with that in mind. He would lead him away from the village, away from this house, follow the canals out of town, then fade into the briar patches along the road to Overloon. But always, Pieter would leave enough of a trail to follow. But where would he go? He'd decide that later, if there was a later.

Before he left, Pieter wrote a brief note to Mama, telling her what to do if he didn't come back by morning. Then, after it was completely dark, he slipped out the back door and headed for the village square. As he stopped to glance back occasionally, he saw no shadows that weren't supposed to be there. But Pieter knew he was being followed. The traitor had been clever enough to hide both his presence and his identity all this time. And he was doing it still.

Hare and hounds, Pieter thought.

Another game that he had played with Koos when they were small. Then he had played that he was one of the hounds, but this time, there was no doubt that he was the hare.

CHAPTER 17

A Desperate Decision

Minutes later

Pieter moved quickly to the center of the village, and soon the *burgemeester's* grand brick house and yard came into view. Once it had been the scene of holiday parties for the villagers given by the wealthy family. Now they lived in a rundown house at the edge of town while Nazi soldiers sprawled in the family's former splendor. As Pieter stopped to study the house for a moment, he could see fancy lace curtains still hanging in the windows. But they looked dirty and torn, even in this dim light.

The house was dark, but Pieter knew that at least one soldier would be on guard duty. Pieter's nerves were raw with fear, yet he forced himself to wait until he saw the soldier round a corner of the house, pause to light a cigarette, and inhale deeply. Then the soldier went on.

As soon as he was out of sight, Pieter moved

quickly to the backyard, pausing near the hawthorn hedge. Once he felt convinced there was no other soldier on patrol, he ran across the dark yard to the garden shed in the far corner. Even the *burgemeester's* shed sagged now, and the door looked as if it would fall off at any moment. The Germans must think that no one would dare steal from them, Pieter thought angrily.

Pieter stepped inside and saw his and Jan's bicycles leaning against the wall. He wasn't really surprised to see his bike after what Beppie had told him the night they sent Jacob's message. Now he wondered what had become of her bike. Was a German officer's wife riding it? Tires, real tires, on these bikes. Even if they were German, they would make the ride easier. For a second Pieter thought of puncturing the tires on Jan's bike, then decided against it. He wanted the traitor to be able to use it if he hadn't brought his own.

Pieter wheeled his bicycle to the door, wishing he had more time to enjoy this moment of stealing his own bike back from the Moffen patrol. That would come later, after the war. Now he waited until the soldier passed by once again. Then Pieter quickly wheeled his bicycle across the yard to the road beyond, which headed to Overloon. Was he being followed? When he glanced back, he saw a shadow on a bike moving behind him, far away but close enough. Good.

Once on the highway, Pieter began to pedal faster. What time was it? A glance upward told him the moon was three-quarters of a silver guilder in size and nearly overhead. But he'd never learned to tell time from the places of the moon or stars in the sky. Had the clock struck eleven or twelve before he left? He had to be finished with all this before dawn.

Slowly he realized he hadn't passed a single person in the half hour or so he'd been on the road. Curfew kept the Dutch indoors, but where were the Germans who had rumbled by in their trucks last week? And the soldiers on the train? A battle soon, no doubt of that.

The thought stabbed him. He could be riding into a huge battle, yet he couldn't turn around. But the traitor could. He could go straight back to the village and expose Mama and Jacob to the Nazis.

Pieter was trapped, and he knew it. He had to name the traitor now, not later, when he returned to the village. And with Beppie gone, there was only one other person who would know what to do with this information. Auntie Riek. He had to go to Auntie Riek and take the traitor with him. Deliver him just the way he'd delivered the ration cards. He'd been headed this way all along.

But he needed time. He needed to be far enough ahead of the traitor to warn Auntie Riek. Then she could make other plans to keep from being exposed if it turned out that the traitor had some way of contacting the Nazis when he realized where Pieter was going.

He picked at his idea like a hen picking over grain hulls. Would it work? Had he forgotten anything? What could he do to give Auntie Riek time to plan, too? Then it came to him.

It was simple. Pieter just had to stall the traitor. Ride around through the brambles, through the woods, up and down the roads until he wore him out, slowed him down in the middle of the forest. Once Pieter got far enough ahead, he could go on to Auntie Riek's, leaving just enough of a trail the traitor could follow. Then Auntie Riek could take over, and Pieter could go home and wait for the war to end. It couldn't come too soon.

Faint, low sounds rumbled in the distance. Not thunder, but man-made sounds. Engines again, the tanks and trucks that he had seen last week. Had to be. Pieter shuddered and nearly lost his balance. He stopped, adjusted his bicycle seat, glanced over his shoulder. Yes, he was still there, a small, blurry shadow.

Pieter rode on until the woods suddenly loomed in the pearly moonlight. He turned his bicycle into the briars at the edge of the forest and fought his way along a path, remembering his brother's talk about lazy afternoons spent just beyond in a meadow, picking berries and kissing girls. One day, maybe. . . .

Nettles dug into his pant legs as he rode along the narrow, bumpy lane. Gradually the path curved south and west, and if the map in his head held true, the Venray turnoff was nearby. He'd come out of the woods close to a farmer's road. But it was too soon to go to Auntie Riek's yet, too easy for the traitor to follow him there. He'd have to circle beyond the bramble path, go deeper into the forest before he dared move out onto that road.

Pieter stopped, took a few deep breaths, and

rubbed his aching eyes. Suddenly he felt exhausted, limp with weariness. What time was it? Two . . . three? The thought of bed and pillow and quilt. . . . He jerked himself awake and pushed deeper into the woods.

Had he chosen the right thing to do? Doubts pummeled him like winter rain. Have I done too much or not enough? What else could I have done? If only he could have asked or even been told . . . but he had to keep going forward; there was no turning back.

Quickly now, Pieter pulled his bicycle off the brambly path and into the overgrowth. He laid it on the ground, then covered it with leaves. Now he could move faster and more quietly through the tangled ground cover. Speed was his ally now. Daylight would bring German patrols, maybe guns and tanks crashing through here. At the very least, exposure to hostile eyes.

The sounds Pieter heard behind him nearly paralyzed him. Twigs breaking, leaves crackling, brambles snapping. Still there, that was good, but too close, that was not so good. He walked softly, stopped to listen, moved on, then rested to listen some more. His jacket sleeve was torn, and there was a rip in his pants. Pieces of himself left behind to point the way, he thought with a flash of panic. But no more of that; now he had to circle one more time and disappear.

He found the earlier path he'd taken and began to circle back, slowly, quietly, one step, then another, then a pause to listen. Sweat trickled down his chest. Fear did that — made you hot, trembly, ready to jump out of your skin. Was this how an animal felt when it was being tracked? He'd never do it again, never scare anybody, never . . . what was that? His breath hurt in his chest. It was stuck; he'd never get it out.

A bird in a tree above him stirred on a branch, and Pieter sagged with relief. Would that bird be here tomorrow? Maybe, maybe not. Where would it go if fighting started here? Would the terrible sounds of war drive the bird away forever?

Slowly, Pieter became aware of the immense silence surrounding him. Now he'd heard nothing for so long that it weighed down on him, making him worry even more. But he had no time for doubts now; he had to keep going. Pieter rushed out of the underbrush, heading for the Venray turnoff road, leaving his bicycle behind. He didn't dare go back for it in case the traitor had found it and was waiting for him.

Half an hour later, he hurried breathlessly up the gravelly path to Auntie Riek's house, bounded up the porch steps, and tapped urgently on the door. Quickly, as if someone had heard or seen him, a key turned in the lock and the door opened a sliver's width. Henk stared at Pieter as if he'd never seen him before.

"I've come to see Auntie Riek," Pieter said.

"We weren't expecting anyone."

"But I must see her. Quickly."

"Who is it?" Pieter heard Auntie Riek's voice behind the door.

Henk turned and spoke a few quiet words. Why didn't they let him come in? "Please," Pieter said.

Henk opened the door enough for Pieter to squeeze inside before he locked it again.

Auntie Riek stood in the doorway of the back parlor where Pieter had last seen her. She wore a dark robe and held a knitting bag and some large balls of yarn in her hands. "Were you followed?"

"Yes. I got rid of him, but only for a while. He's coming, but there's time . . ."

"What did you do?"

Pieter rushed to explain. "I circled round and round in the woods to wear him out, slow him down. First, I let him follow me from the village so that he wouldn't find the American soldier in my house. But I couldn't let him go back. He's the one — the traitor from our village. My mother would have been arrested. . . . I didn't know what else to do."

"I understand." Auntie Riek spoke softly and slowly.

Henk suddenly put a finger to his lips. "Someone's outside," he whispered. Then he pointed to the doorknob. It turned slowly, first this way, then that. He'd come too soon, Pieter realized with horror. Still hare and hounds. Pieter was still the hare, but now he'd been run to the ground and there was no place to go.

CHAPTER 18

A Traitor Exposed

A heartbeat later

"Unlock the door. Let him come in." Auntie Riek stood there, so calm, so quiet.

"No!" Pieter cried out. What was wrong with her? Didn't she understand who was out there?

Auntie Riek motioned for him to be silent, then nodded to Henk. He turned the key in the lock, and the door opened. Pieter didn't want to look at the man who stepped inside, but he had to face him now.

Had this been the right thing to do? Yes, he had to believe that it was. Now Mama was safe, and Jacob too, unless the traitor had others back in the village that he'd trained, that were sympathetic, that would — No, no, he couldn't think that.

Pieter looked away at first, then turned, knowing he had to look at Jan's father, look him square in the face. It meant facing those unwelcome thoughts about Mr. de Waard — and realizing he had misjudged other people. Even his strongest suspicion about Mr. van der Meer had been only that and nothing more.

"Mr. de Waard! Why, why?" he asked. How would Jan live with the knowledge that his father was a traitor? Or had Jan figured it out and been unsure what to do about it? That could explain the way he'd acted lately.

"How could you do this to your family, to us, your friends? We trusted you!" Pieter heard the anguish in his own voice.

"I don't expect you to understand yet," Mr. de Waard said. "You're too young."

"Don't say that!" Pieter shouted. "I'm not too young to understand between right and wrong. Neither is Jan."

At the mention of Jan's name, Mr. de Waard's shoulders slumped, and for a moment he looked as if he would fall. Pieter took a step toward him.

"Stay where you are." Mr. de Waard's voice was different now, cold, like an icy rush of North Sea wind. And something else was different, too. In his right hand he held a gun, which he used to gesture toward Auntie Riek.

"I have come for my prize," he said. "There is quite a price on your head, old woman."

"Auntie Riek?" Pieter couldn't believe it. "But she only . . ."

"She is the commander of the Resistance for over half of Holland," Mr. de Waard said. He smiled, but it was the smile of a ferret.

"Close the door, Henk." Auntie Riek still hadn't moved.

Mr. de Waard hooted with laughter. "You expect me to believe that there's someone behind me? Try again."

"As you wish," she answered.

Pieter couldn't breathe. Mr. de Waard seemed to be in charge — he had the gun — but Auntie Riek refused to move. Did she think that Henk and he were going to save her? But they were just kids, no match for this man.

Mr. de Waard gestured with his gun again. "I'm tired of this game. Let's go."

Pieter knew they had to do something. Henk must have sensed it too, because suddenly he slammed the door. At the same instant, Pieter jumped toward Mr. de Waard, who was surprisingly limber. In one movement he swung at Pieter, knocking him to the floor, then turned and kicked Henk on the chin, who collapsed like rubble.

Pieter started to get up. "Don't move," Mr. de Waard ordered, pointing his gun straight at Pieter.

A sharp noise, like the backfire of Uncle Bro's old truck, reverberated around the room until the sound exploded in Pieter's ears. He noticed the surprised look on Mr. de Waard's face as he slowly crumpled to the floor.

Pieter turned to stare at Auntie Riek. He saw the gun in her hand, protruding from a ball of yarn. "Is he . . . Did you . . ."

"Yes, Pieter." She sounded so sad. "It had to be."

He shook his head, trying to clear it of his confusion. "He said you were . . ."

"The Nazis consider me important," she answered, moving quickly to Henk now. "Please, help me put him in this chair."

They eased Henk into a sitting position, and Auntie Riek examined the ugly bruise already developing on his chin. "He will be all right in a few minutes," she said.

"Where's Beppie?" Pieter asked, trying to make Henk more comfortable.

"She went to Overloon, but I expect her back any moment."

"I'll watch for her." As Pieter turned to the door, he confronted Mr. de Waard's body lying so still in his traitor's blood. Suddenly the room began to spin, and Pieter felt as if he would faint. He'd never seen anyone die before, not even in all the years of war.

Auntie Riek was beside him, her arm around his shoulders. "Death is never easy, Pieter, even when it's the enemy who dies."

Pieter shook violently. "He was Jan's pa, my best friend's father, and I led him here. It's my fault."

"No, Pieter, he followed you because he chose the side of the Nazis. We're free to make choices in our lives, but then we have to take the responsibility for them."

"Someone's coming." Henk was sitting up straight now.

Jan. Could Jan have followed his father?

Auntie Riek hurried to stand beside the door as it opened, the gun still in her hand.

Beppie stepped inside. "German soldiers coming

this way," she said breathlessly. She looked at Pieter before glancing down at Mr. de Waard's body. Quickly she came to Pieter's side and hugged him. "Hold on," she whispered. "You did the right thing."

"How many soldiers?" Auntie Riek asked Beppie.

"Three or four. In the barn across the road." Beppie took a breath before she went on. "I think they heard the shot that did this." She gestured to Mr. de Waard's body. "Come on. We've got to get out of here."

Pieter strained to hear the sound of soldiers' footsteps outside. Instead he heard another sound that he knew from a time long ago. "I heard a dog whining."

"The soldiers' truck has a large wire cage on the back of it." Beppie helped Henk stand up. "There must be six or eight dogs inside it."

"Dogs?" Pieter asked. "What are they doing with guard dogs?"

Beppie turned to him. "They're not guard dogs. In Overloon, they talk of nothing else but a battle that's being formed east of here, in the woods. The Germans are going to make a stand against the Allies and our Resistance."

"The dogs have been trained to sniff out mines," Auntie Riek went on. "But if some of the dogs make a mistake, the Germans can always find more somewhere."

Pieter tried not to think about Auntie Riek's words. Just tried to concentrate on his next move. "Where is the truck, exactly?"

"Halfway between here and the barn," Beppie said.

"I'll divert them long enough for the rest of you to get out," he said. "Is there a back door?"

"Through there," Beppie began. "But you can't do it alone."

"I'm going to try," Pieter said. "When you hear the dogs bark really loud, run out the back door and head for home." He couldn't believe what he'd just proposed. He sounded so sure of himself — not at all how he felt inside.

Pieter looked at each of them for a moment, hoping he'd meet Auntie Riek and Henk again, after the war. He hoped to see Beppie for the rest of his life, if they survived.

He slipped out of the house, then crept behind a tree to watch and wait and listen. In the distance he heard the chatter of guns answered by dull artillery thuds. As his eyes became accustomed to the darkness, he saw three shadows emerge from a barn doorway. Then cones of light appeared as three German soldiers moved slowly toward Auntie Riek's house. But Beppie said there were four. Could one be with the truck?

Pieter hurried around the house, then crawled into a field of grass along the edge of the yard. He stayed low to the ground until he judged the truck was no more than a meter or two away from him. Then, cautiously, he stood. The truck appeared to be empty. He approached slowly, hearing the dogs turn in their cages as they sensed his nearness. Pieter hadn't even dared to think of Kazan until now. Was it possible? Dared he hope that his dog would be here?

Gravel crunched under the soldiers' boots as they

neared Auntie Riek's front porch. No more time to wonder or hope or be afraid. Quickly Pieter ran alongside the truck to the back and found the wire door to the cage, but he couldn't pry it open. A rusty pin in the clasp wouldn't give way.

One of the dogs snarled suddenly and tried to grab Pieter's hand. Pieter hit the cage hard and drove the dog back, away from the door. The other dogs moved back too, whining, growling, panting furiously. Surely the soldiers had heard the dogs now.

He tried again, driving the pin into the palm of his hand, wincing when he threw open the door. The dogs leaped past him, barking wildly as they ran down the road and disappeared from view.

The soldiers shouted and turned their flashlights in Pieter's direction. He leaped into the tall grass, dropped to his knees, and drew in deep breaths that hurt his throat. Gradually the shouting of the soldiers faded in the distance as they ran in the other direction, pursuing the dogs. Beppie and the others should be safely out of the house now, hiding or starting home. Good. In a moment, he could start for home, too.

Pieter tensed as the grass began to move nearby. Who was it? Something touched his hand briefly, gave it a tentative lick, drew away, then touched it again with a soft, damp nose. A whimper, then a whisper of tail brushing grass.

For a heartbeat, Pieter didn't look down so he could believe for that brief moment that it was Kazan. But it wasn't. It was a skinny brown dog from the truck, probably tired of the war, wanting to go home, too.

"Shhh," Pieter whispered, stretching out his hand to the dog and stroking its fur. They listened together for sounds they didn't want to hear.

After several long, agonizing minutes, Pieter stood up and glanced around. Everyone was gone. Soldiers, friends, even dogs. Except for one.

The noise came without warning. Grass snapped underfoot, the dog growled, the safety clasp on a gun unfastened.

"Halt!"

Pieter turned to stare at the German soldier pointing a flashlight and a pistol at him. He couldn't see the soldier's face, but he heard a voice that was not young.

"You are alone?" He spoke good Dutch.

"Yes." Pieter barely spoke aloud.

The soldier hesitated, took several steps closer, still holding the gun on Pieter. "You are not very old."

"I am thirteen." Now he could see that many lines mapped an old face under a cap's visor. Uniform tunic buttoned over a bratwurst belly.

"My grandson was twelve. A bomb killed him," the soldier said.

"I am sorry. But what are you going to do with me?" Should he beg? "My mother, she's alone. She needs me." And suddenly Pieter needed her. He was a little boy again, and he wanted the comfort of his mother nearby.

Slowly the soldier lowered his gun to his side and shrugged. "Would it bring my grandson back if I were to shoot you? Would we win the war by taking one more life?" He shook his head. "Take your dog and go home."

Pieter couldn't move. It was a trick. As soon as he began to run, the soldier would gun him down. Hares and hounds again. Would the game never end?

"Go on, before I remember I'm supposed to be a soldier." He gestured with his weapon.

Pieter turned then and began to run through the grass, fear pounding him senseless. He couldn't think or even question or hope. He just ran, stumbling over clumps of grass, dirt, and rock, feeling his breath clot in his throat, tasting its sour backwash, feeling saliva drip down his chin, waiting to hear the whine of a bullet that would spread death inside him.

Then he fell, and his mouth filled with the taste of the field, his nose filled with the rich scents of earth and the stench of the war dog who flopped beside him. My last moment alive, Pieter thought, and waited to die.

But nothing happened. Slowly he raised his head and looked directly into the eyes of the dog lying beside him. "We're still alive," Pieter whispered, and took deep breaths of the night air as if to prove it to himself.

He got up on his knees in time to see the old soldier climbing stiffly into the truck. Not all Dutchmen are good, Pieter thought, remembering Mr. de Waard. Nor are all Germans bad.

"Let's go," he said to the dog, and then stood up. "There's work to be done before Papa and my brothers get home from the war." They began to walk slowly, quietly, taking care that they were alone.

Pieter was convinced that his brothers and Papa would come home, and that soon life would be as it had been before the war. Papa would smoke his pipe by the fireplace, watching as Gerrit teased Mama and told his jokes. Menno soon would have girlfriends all around town, just as Pieter would have Beppie as his one and only girlfriend.

And everyone would want to hear about the American soldier and what became of him. Pieter would explain that Jacob returned to his regiment and went home after the war. Did he have a girlfriend waiting for him? And a dog, too?

And Kazan? Would he find his way home? Pieter had to believe with all his heart that one day . . . one day. . . .

"When Kazan comes home, you'll have to share his bed," Pieter told the dog walking beside him. "But it's yours in the meantime. Come on, let's go home. If we hurry, we can be there by sunrise."

Afterword

The battle of Overloon occurred as a result of military maneuvers that began on September 17, 1944, when Allied paratroopers landed at Oosterbeek, sixty kilometers to the north. After this maneuver, the German military decided to move south and establish a new front along the Maas River.

Patrol activities by both sides intensified. On September 27, Germans occupying Overloon evacuated the local residents to avert heavy civilian losses. Allied bombardment began at midnight.

Several days later, a tank battle erupted in and around the village. At first, German tanks controlled the fight, causing the Allies, particularly the U.S. troops, to withdraw. But the following week, the Allies' British troops advanced through the town, securing it in house-by-house combat. When the British finally occupied the ruins of the church, the Germans fled into the woods and continued fighting along the road to Venray. The battle of Overloon ended on October 16, 1944.

In May 1946, one year after the war ended in Europe, a museum was opened on the battlefield outside Overloon. Soldiers who took part in the war donated a variety of artifacts — such as hand weapons, uniforms, medals, and photographs — that have been placed on permanent exhibit in the museum building. Larger remnants of the fight, including weapons and war vehicles, have been left outside where the actual fighting took place. The author researched this book at the museum and spoke to survivors about their experiences. Their memories have been handed down to succeeding generations as a reminder of the consequences of war.

PRONUNCIATION GUIDE

Arnhem	ARN-hem
Baron	Bah-RONE (o as in only)
Boxmeer	Box-MI-UR (i as in it)
burgemeester	BURGUH-mayster
de Jong	duh YONG
de Waard	duh VAHRD
Dorthwijk	Dorth-WIKE
Gerda	GER-dah (er as in error)
Gerrit	GER-rit
Henk	HENK
Huishoud	HISE-haut
Jan	YAHN
klompen	KLOM-pen (o as in only)
Kooiman	KOY-mahn
Koos	KOSE
Lida	LEE-dah
Maas	MAHS
Moffen	MOF-fen (o as in only)
Oosterbeek	Oaster-BAKE
Overloon	Oaver-LONE
Pieter	PE-ter
Prager	PRAH-ger
Riek	RE'K (e as in deliver)
van der Meer	vahn der MI-UR (i as in it)
van Dijk	vahn DIKE
van Dirk	vahn DIRK (i as in it)
van Hal	vahn HAHL
Venray	Ven-RYE

133